BOZUK

BOZUK

LINDA ROGERS

Publishers of Singular
Fiction, Poetry, Nonfiction, Drama, Translations and Graphic Books

Library and Archives Canada Cataloguing in Publication

Rogers, Linda, 1944-, author
Bozuk / Linda Rogers.

Issued in print and electronic formats.
ISBN 978-1-55096-597-1 (paperback).--ISBN 978-1-55096-598-8 (epub).
--ISBN 978-1-55096-600-8 (mobi).--ISBN 978-1-55096-602-2 (pdf)

I. Title

PS8585.O392B69 2016   C813'.54   C2016-904878-0
                                                            C2016-904879-9

Design and Composition by Mishi Uroboros
Typeset in Big Caslon, Lucida Grande, Ceria Lebaran, Minion,
Futura and Constantia fonts at Moons of Jupiter Studios

Published by Exile Editions Ltd ~ www.ExileEditions.com
144483 Southgate Road 14 – GD, Holstein, Ontario, N0G 2A0
Printed on Laid paper, and bound in Canada in 2016, by Marquis

We gratefully acknowledge, for their support toward our publishing
activities, the Canada Council for the Arts, the Government of Canada,
the Ontario Arts Council, and the Ontario Media Development Corporation.

Canadian sales: The Canadian Manda Group, 664 Annette Street,
Toronto ON M6S 2C8 www.mandagroup.com 416 516 0911

North American and International Distribution, and U.S. Sales:
Independent Publishers Group, 814 North Franklin Street,
Chicago IL 60610   www.ipgbook.com   toll free: 1 800 888 4741

For Olive: peace, deep roots, and laughter.

For Mandoturk, Jack and Eva,
Sweet Papa Lowdown and the Pinks
(Naomi, Hannah and Françoise):
Ne mutlu Türküm diyene

and our Turkish family, especially Luisa Galata Dinc,
born in the shade of Gezi Parki:

*There's a blaze of light
in every word.
It doesn't matter which you heard,
the holy or the broken hallelujah.*
— LEONARD COHEN, "Hallelujah"

The visionary is the only true realist.
— FEDERICO FELLINI

SENDE ANTA/TELL YOUR STORY

Madeleine, sometimes known as Maddy, but more often as Mad, travels to Turkey during the Arab Spring and finds Pamuk's snow, which had promised wisdom, the voice of God, has frozen the green shoots and modern conversations about inclusion and secular democracy.

Moderate Turks have since risen up, like the angel mosaics emerging from plaster shrouds in the Aya Sofia, to protect trees filled with singing birds in Gesi Park and the rights of women – some of them marching in skirts. Now that Equinox has transitioned to a winter of real discontent, what started as peaceful debate has exploded in horrible statistics. Women in Turkey are now ten times more likely to endure violence.

The key word is "permission" and it began with the terrorism defined as government repression of human rights. Some Turkish men who had given hard glances to women who uncovered their heads or those who carried schoolbooks now believe they have permission to rape and murder anyone who transgresses their brutal medievalist interpretation of Islam.

Imam, the Libyan lawyer who was gang-raped by Gaddafi's soldiers, and Malala, the child advocate, are no longer exceptional examples of religion gone wrong.

We have heard of the brutal murders at the Ankara train station and Sultanahmet, and of Ozgecan Aslan, a nineteen-year-old Turkish university student whose crimes were going to school and resisting rape. She was stabbed and beaten, her head broken, *bozuk*,* and burned, her charred remains left in a riverbed.

Ozgecan's blackened remains dissolve in music. Millions of mourning women exchanging photos on social media sing like blackbirds. Will the world listen to the unacceptability of cruelty and plant an olive tree for every martyr, fill every woman-shaped grave with hope?

* A Glossary of Turkish words appears on pages 234 and 235

ONCE I PLAYED GOD

We had a dog. His name was Fred but I called him Frend. I told him all my troubles, for example, my parents wouldn't let me wear nail polish until I quit sucking my thumb. I didn't get pie and ice cream until I finished my cold and lumpy mashed potatoes.

Once, when my father sent me to my room for some small transgression of the dad laws, I yelled at my door, "I hope the sky falls down on you!" – never thinking it would. Sometimes, before our life changed forever, I imagined them both struck by lightning, but God decides.

It is wrong to take a life. I have never done that on purpose, even though people keep dying on me like the grasshopper I kept in a glass jar with breathing holes and a dandelion bed. I got a needle and thread and made him the tiniest pair of pants and a little shirt.

Since Frend was officially my parents' dog, he slept in their bed not mine. The grasshopper was mine exclusively. He rubbed his leg against his belly and talked to me. When I took him out of his jar and he tried to escape, I took the sewing scissors and cut off his leg. Good idea, I thought, but the next morning he was dead.

WHY ON EARTH

After the sky fell, I asked my bereaved mother why she was in such a hurry to get to the end of every last jug of gin in the western world. She told me an angel, aka Dad, left messages in the heels of her bottles. You had to tip the sucker right up to the sun to see. You had to swallow the in-between, whether you liked the taste of it or not. I didn't believe her about the messages, but I do have the same need not only to get to the bottom of things but also to the top, the Olympian summits where gods and holy choirs hang out.

My mother and I both believed that my father had become one of them. A long time ago, I asked him to teach me the names of all the stars and all the planets. "That's my Earth," I told him when he showed me a map of our solar system. "You can't have The Earth," he said. "No one can have the whole world; but we can catch you some fallen stars that'll be all your own."

The next Saturday, it rained. He went out to the garden and hung bottles on our monkey tree. My mother and I stood in the living-room window and watched him.

"Your father's gone loco," she said, but I already knew monkey trees were sacred.

"Monkey trees are for wishing," he told me when he'd planted it. "Whenever you see one, pinch the person closest to you and say a prayer."

The closest person was my mother. Her real name was Estelle but my dad called her Stella, which means "star" in Italian. Sometimes he pinched her and said he'd already got his wish. That was true and not true, as it turned out, the usual bullshit. My father had big soft lips. When he kissed my eyes goodnight, he said he was spitting stardust on them; and I believed him.

Sunday morning, the sun was out. My father blindfolded me and led me down the front stairs. He stood me right by the monkey tree and uncovered my eyes. I saw sparkle and swirling blues, yellows, purples and greens. I heard tinkling, and Daddy said it was angels speaking in the bottles hanging from the branches of the monkey tree.

"This is your galaxy," he said. "Wish on these stars. Make all the wishes you want."

He said the bottles would catch the bad spirits before they came in our house, but he was wrong. Some bad spirits took my daddy away and my mother invited the rest to stay. After he was gone she insisted that gin lifted her spirits. That was wishful thinking. Hers were as heavy as lead.

Stella never did find a message from Daddy or any other angel in one of her bottles. When the gin fairies finally got her, I put on the jet choker she'd worn after he died. She told me the necklace had belonged to my great-great granny. "It's my consolation," she'd said, touching the shiny black beads as if they were her rosary. "Jet's made from petrified monkey tree." Maybe she pinched it all night long, wishing my dad back after the pinch fairies carried him off.

The spirit tree was my consolation. When I heard my bottles banging in the wind, I knew he was speaking to me. The problem was I was too grief-shocked to understand what he was saying. Now I have hung bottles from the branches of every tree in our garden. That's my hunger. I can't stop doing it. I have to believe that someday my father will tell me why on earth my life in this world has turned out this way.

The Prostitute

At least fifteen men raped her, she alleges. Then they pissed and shat on her. The Libyan government does not agree. The military does not agree.

The local press does not agree. Her family does not agree with the government, the military or the local press. Her mother says Iman wanted to study journalism but there is no freedom of expression in Libya. Instead she studied law. That way, maybe she could join the struggle for human rights.

Does a Muslim lawyer wear red nail polish, the world is left to wonder. Does a lawyer belly dance, they infer from a photo of someone else, a young woman with all ten fingers.

Somehow Iman managed to be born with only nine or else she'd lost one in an accident, perhaps chopping vegetables for her family or tilting a windmill. Do they have windmills in Libya? Did the winds of change bring Iman into the light so we would witness what happens when we don't pay attention to the lives of girls and women?

Avaraz is collecting a million signatures on a petition to free Iman, who is under house arrest in Tripoli for the crime of being raped. They are going to present the list to president Erdoğan of Turkey and ask him to intervene since he was able to negotiate the release of four *New York Times* journalists held in Libyan jails. I signed the petition and bought a ticket to Istanbul because I need to understand why women suffer, or, more to the point, to understand if God is responsible for allowing us to take the rap for mankind's inevitable failures. Is this the snake biting our heels, another variation on original sin, the story at the root of everything wrong with this world? It is just a story, isn't it, the story of mankind and my own family, which allegedly came from the ancient city of Smyrna, the source of myrrh taken by a wise man to celebrate the birth of the son of God so that he might die for our sins?

I always thought God was incredibly stupid to go to all the trouble of making a child just so he could suffer. I am against war and gods who ask for the sacrifice of children. I am against scriptures that degrade women and men who would be women. I always thought Jesus was gay and had an extraordinary sympathy for women. Is that why they nailed him to a tree?

AIMAN'S MOTHER

I saw Iman's mother on television this morning She had that coiled furious look snakes have when "resting," their half-shut eyes glittering, the muscle that holds the jawbone to the head bone twitching, waiting for an opportunity to bite and swallow. Given the chance, Iman's mother will tear the heads off the soldiers who abducted and abused her daughter in Tripoli. She threatened to strangle Gaddafi.

Iman's mother will close her eyes and see a line of green uniforms, soldiers waiting their turn to violate her daughter. I know it, just as surely as I know I will see her face glowing in the dark when I turn out the light tonight. She will not blink until the last soldier is turned back at the gate to Paradise. Iman's mother will stare down God to avenge her child.

NOW

When I was an unhappy kid with an abdicated mother and no friends, I lost myself in books, reading all day and all night. I wasn't interested in school, so my teachers gave up teaching me. They let me sit at the back of the class and read, the idea being, I suppose, that I was maybe an autodidact and something positive might come from doing classroom time so long as they left me alone to learn in my own way. No one signed my report cards. No one came to PTA meetings or teacher-parent interviews. I became invisible and silent except for the sound of turning pages. At night I sat up in bed and read until I fell asleep. No one came to tuck me in or turn out the lamp. No one warned me that I was hurting my eyes and missing my beauty sleep.

I was a lump of white bread with dirty hair and fingernails. Beauty came later. My real life was and is fiction. Even after my metamorphosis from fat kid to real woman, a well-informed comforter on call to pleasure elders, reading is still my number one escape and pleasure. Riding the bus, waiting for clients, waiting for rest, I read. They should put a statue of me reading in front of the public library. I am their best customer.

I read all of Sir Walter Scott and Shakespeare. I walked right into the workhouses of Dickens's London. Those poor kids were just like me – orphans and misfits, struggling to survive in a world of losers and drunks. I read Homer, my father's illustrated *Iliad* and *Odyssey*, and mind-travelled to Asia Minor, imagining the spectacular rosy-fingered dawn I have just now seen rising out of the Aegean Sea. I laughed and I cried as Penelope, Portia, and Tiny Tim walked into my head and told their stories.

I came to Asia Minor riding the magic carpet that carried me over the rough terrain of my childhood to lands beyond imagining. That ancestral carpet is a bit worn now, but it still lifts my spirits. It may lift me to the pinnacle of the steepest and highest mountain in this western Turkey. I have a fear of heights, but I have ridden the magic carpet all my life, so I trust it when there is nothing else to rely on.

According to my mother, who read an article about Ephesus in a travel magazine, my father was not Italian as his family alleged, but Turkish. Our last name, Turka, is Italian for Turkish. I suppose I began to read Turkish poems and stories because digging for our roots would make up for losing him before I was ready to be transplanted to the land of alien mothers. I learned that famine and disease forced half the Lydian population to migrate. My ancestors may have been among them.

Eventually my investigation brought me to Orhan Pamuk. His novel *Snow* took forever to read. Many times I almost stopped. The realities were painful, the politics frightening and divisive. His enigmatic characters frustrated me, especially the contradictory sisters who, I now understand, represent the secular and religious realities of a country besieged on every physical and ideological border and violated by countless external influences. I identified with both of them and would have given anything for a sibling.

Ka, Pamuk's fictitious poet, who embraces every reality, the saints and whores of his confused civilization, had his ta-dah! moment. He heard God in the silence of snow. I was dying to go and listen for whatever Turkey could teach me, but I had no spare change, what the Turks call *bozuk para*.

Then Mr. Good-one died and I got a sweet package deal.

How did this happen? The short answer is that Mr. Gudewill (who came out with a surprised and happy "good one!" bless him, every time he came) was very good to me. In exchange for comfort, he insisted on paying me twice my usual charge of twenty bucks an hour, all services included. Because I wasn't employed by his rest home, I hadn't signed the "no tip" agreement.

My good one gave me a big bonus at the end, but his greatest gift was friendship with a real person. I'm not saying there is anything wrong with the angel conversations my father started, but I have been lonely in the in-between.

Every patient gets to bring a few of their favourite things to care facilities. The ladies usually chose a chair or family photos. Mr. Gudewill brought his library. Because he was so nice to the staff – peeling twenties they were required by law to return, off the stack in his drawer – the cleaners and nurses worked around his piles of books, leaving them undisturbed.

I allowed extra time for my sessions with Mr. Gudewill; and afterward we drank tea and talked about the books I borrowed from him and read carefully because he kept his books in pristine condition. We debated whether or not dementia patients like Hagar in *The Stone Angel* should be allowed to wander, even at their peril, why Jane Austen failed to accuse the slave-trading sea captains preening in her drawing rooms, if Murasaki Shikibu was recognized as the first Japanese novelist because she wrote in her own dialect, unlike the men in her circle who imitated the Chinese style, and if Andre Aciman's seder at the end of *Out of Egypt* wasn't the pinnacle of post-Holocaust literature. No one had talked to me like that since my dad went to Heaven with all his special opinions.

Mr. Gudewill agreed with me that women writers were underrated, and he always listened respectfully to my opinions. He was my university. Because I was introverted and passed as thick, no one else noticed I had a brain. Mr. Gudewill and I had a love affair with books. The sex part was purely functional, my rule and his preference.

Mr. Gudewill had a daughter, Sandra. He called her "Princess." She was not pleased with his new wife, a card shark from Vegas. He told me honestly that he wanted sex and she wanted money, which he had a lot of, having been a successful stockbroker.

Before his bride turned up to argue with the child of his earlier marriage about who got which antique or valuable painting, he handed me an envelope and told me not to open it until he was with the angels.

Inside was a letter in shaky handwriting, thanking me for my companionship and a stack of life-changing thousand-dollar bills. One hundred thousand dollars! I might have been obliged to inform his wife if she had behaved decently, but, to the best of my knowledge, she had never shown him a shred of respect before I'd called to inform her he was on his way out. She only phoned to ask for money.

Since I inherited my parents' house, debt free, my income allows for a comfortable life without frills. My needs are simple: books, food, and a bottle of wine that lasts a week because I am still the adult child of an alcoholic, and I only drink the one or two glasses of daily red that is recommended for heart health. That is good wine though. I don't drink plonk. The wine in Turkey is ordinary. I prefer *raki*, the anise-flavoured aperitif they mix with water and drink with the *mezzes* that start their meals.

Poor Mr. Gudewill, who had been wise in business and had great taste in literature, was helpless in lust. "I am not a real gambler," he said. "I've seen the Northern Lights and I've seen Paris at night. I wanted to witness Sodom lit up. In one weekend, I met and married a girl who worked in a casino. I took Viagra. The sex was great. I bought her a house. She said she was going to follow me home to Victoria as soon as her immigration papers were straightened out. We'd spend summers here and winters in Vegas."

It turned out she had a boyfriend and a teenaged son. "As soon as I left Vegas, they all moved into the house I'd bought for us."

Mr. Gudewill told me he didn't mind so much about the other man swimming in his pool. Since there was an age difference, he understood; but he wished she would visit from time to time. "I miss the sex." If I didn't know better, I would have asked, "At your age, Mr. Gudewill?" Just as young soldiers lie dying on the battleground, calling for their mothers, I know from experience that old men often die with the name of the last woman they've slept with on their lips.

Not Mr. Gudewill, who called out to the mother of his child on his way out. The next day, I bought my ticket to Istanbul with cash.

On the second leg of the flight, from Frankfurt to Istanbul, I sat near the members of a Canadian blues band who were about to play clubs and resorts on the Aegean and Mediterranean coasts, Sweet Papa Lowdown and family, two daughters and two wives. This band – Jeff, a guitarist; Rick, a mandolinist; Doug, a tenor sax player and Kris, on trombone – was joining Turkish musicians, more new friends. "How appropriate," I said, "A fusion band in a fusion country." They liked that I had done my political homework and offered me comps for any concert I could find, which turned out to be harder than we thought because directions are Byzantine in Turkey. I didn't say I was fusion too, because I have come to simplify, just as the Turks have been doing for almost a century, only they call it, "secularization."

"I sometimes work with a band," I said after we made introductions, which is sort of a lie and almost true. When I am seeing clients who prefer the anonymity at the storage locker, a habit I haven't changed even after my mother declined, clearing a room in our house, I like the background music. It helps my work.

"I came to hear snow and witness the rescue of Iman al-Obeidi," I said, leaving out the part about my father, my full agenda, "but I like the blues."

"Same key," Kris said.

The Harem

The moment I arrived in Istanbul, I understood why Pamuk would hear his God as opposed to seeing him.

I have discovered that Istanbul is a city of unique music, from the first cry of the muezzin calling the faithful to morning prayer, the mating of feral cats, the cuckoo coo of the ubiquitous doves and the elegant crow doves, with grey breasts and black heads and wings, to the soulful groove of the *saz* player who makes magic with his Turkish stringed instrument in a doorway on the empty İstiklal Caddesi after all the nightlife on Beyoğlu's lit-up street of dreams has vanished. I understood right away that Turks speak softly, their gently percussive language borrowed from the sounds around them. They don't attempt to dominate like we do. They dissemble and adapt, the grumbling mostly apparent in their humour, seismic activity.

Right away, I felt connected in this country of bridges and ferries and buses that serve snacks and rosewater for cleaning your hands. Almost as soon as I arrived in Istanbul, I became part of a polite human grid with a Byzantine infrastructure.

Even in the manic traffic of this bulging city, the Turks are considerate. I've been here three weeks, blending into the population of thirteen million plus tourists and I haven't seen a single dented car or an incident that escalated into violence, not even shouting, so finding guns for sale in the tunnel shops under the Galata Bridge is disturbing. Because my father was a veteran and a seasonal hunter of wild meat, I got used to seeing weapons around when I was a kid, but this is an anomaly in a country that, like my own, strives to accommodate.

"Why are there so many gun shops under the bridge?" I ask Vefa, the Kadıköy-based Sweet Papa Lowdown bassist who offered to show me the Topkapı Sarayı. "What are the weapons for?"

I expect Vefa, wearing a hoodie and waving an elegant ebony cigarette holder in long fingers, to give me an ambiguous Turkish answer. After all, I have had to dig for personal information. He lives with his parents in an old Ottoman apartment that has belonged to his family for generations. Vefa is a musician who translates philosophical writing and his father's poetry. I heard he was in love, but, like many young Turks, had decided that taking love a step further was too risky in his world, so he remained single.

"We hunt women," he quips and waits for my reaction.

"Why do you need weapons for that?"

"We kill them and eat them."

"How?"

"Turkish women require two days of cooking. They are very tough."

"When is it time to eat them?"

"When they tell the truth."

Ah, that is the power of Turkish women. They dissemble behind their veils and that infuriates their equally enigmatic men. It is always about power and there is no power greater than secrets. Byzantine.

I'm a hunter too, I think, stalking myself. Will I see the person I am looking for quivering like a trapped animal in my father's gunsight, just another confused woman circling the drain?

On our way to the Ottoman Palace in Sultanahmet, we stop in the park and consult the fortune bunnies who choose prophetic notes for tourists.

"Do you also punish the rabbits when they choose unpopular fortunes? "

"Of course.

"There are thirteen million people to feed in Istanbul. So many souls have moved west looking for work, our country is tipping into the Aegean. Rabbits, women, pigeons: it's all about food."

Having come to Turkey to feed my soul, I don't know whether to laugh or punch Vefa's bowing arm.

"Let's spare the rabbit this time," he says, laughing.

I am learning that politics and religion in this country are a powerful mix of mystery and beauty – so much hidden, lost in translation, so much revealed, all of it a joke until it isn't.

Vefa walks quickly. It's hard keeping up with him, keeping an eye on the street life around us, and asking the right questions.

"Why do so many people smoke?"

"We are praying," he answers.

Blowing smoke signals. "Does the Ottoman God allow the dead to smoke in heaven?

"I'll let you know when I get there. This will do for now."

We have arrived at our destination. Light and colour flow from the Topkapı gate, welcoming us to the magnificence inside. Only the intense illustrations in the *Rubaiyat* have prepared me for this exotic visual feast. I swallow my breath. Vefa says nothing, but I feel his smile. Turks, I am noticing, may be critical of their history, but they are proud of it.

He takes my arm and steers me through crowds of visitors. I am amazed at every turn as we navigate the gardens and maze of exquisite buildings. Even the luxurious intimacy of practical spaces like the circumcision room and the library have a celestial glow as we step in and out of what could be medieval paintings.

"Does this confuse you?" he asks, touching my sleeve with his cigarette holder.

"Careful, you'll set me on fire."

"That would be interesting," he says. "A different flavour from boiling for days."

"I didn't come here to be eaten. I came to find people." Isn't that the truth, I think, as he leads me through an arched doorway, everything visible becoming invisible. I am tired of being left behind and would like to hold on to something, somebody, just once.

"And this is where your family might have left you." Vefa leads me through a stone corridor from full Ottoman glory into a morose courtyard. "We are in the harem, where girls waited to be chosen to join the sultan." When he speaks, a gathering of black and grey crows gather their skirts and disappear with a whisper. I have thought, and think again, that these unusual crows, whose dingy headscarves have slipped, are a symbol of assimilation in this diverse culture.

"My father left me with something worse."

"What was that?" he asks.

"My mother."

The harem courtyard could be a prison compound. I shiver, wondering who on earth would consider it a privilege to be selected for the Sultan's pleasure? Who would send a daughter to live in a jail surrounded by so much inaccessible beauty?

We sit down on a stone bench and I think while Vefa, the Byzantine aristocrat who sleeps by himself, puts a cigarette in his holder and just holds it. I reflect about all the little girls who grow up and marry up, attaching their destinies to powerful men. And what happens to them when power turns evil? Are they just innocent passengers on the train to infamy? I think of men who do the same thing fucking with the devil, men like Faust, and Robert Johnson who wanted to sing himself out of the chains of slavery. Iman was so brave to leave her proxy husband behind. I want to carve her name in stone, in this place or, failing that, in my thigh.

"Did the girls in the harem even get to see the gardens?" I ask Vefa, who should be feeling badly about his little jokes. "Only when invited," he laughs, predictably. I suspect the leftover Ottoman princes, to the best of my knowledge all remittance poets, philosophers and musicians disempowered by Ataturk, cultivate their cynicism. Sophistication is their manhood. I'm not fooled. I've seen too many vulnerable men. The ones I've been meeting here are the cultural progeny of the infamous harem eunuchs.

"Do you think they slept with the eunuchs?" I ask, hoping to startle him, and because I have read that Vatican castrati kept neglected Roman noblewomen content; but Vefa is prepared.

"It was all about protecting bloodlines. Why should any slave, man or woman, be cut off from pleasure?"

I am tempted to tell him about my clients, but hold my tongue. This culture is still new to me. "No reason at all. Sex without issue is very modern."

"And necessary," he adds enigmatically and stands up. "Your people know what to do. Arm everyone and shoot people who believe in birth control. That is population control."

"I am not an American. Why does everyone think Canadians are American?"

"Now," he says, ignoring my question, "we will go to the holy of holies."

The Palace could be an encampment, tents rendered in stone. There is nothing grand about the architecture. It is practical, but sumptuous in its appointments, a warehouse for plunder at the end of the Silk Road.

We cross another garden and he leads me to the Sultan's apartment. The rooms are splendid, but I am most impressed by the balcony looking over the Bosphorus. Its stone walls frame stunning tableaux of the water and the ancient city connected by ships.

This is exactly what the potentate saw, I think, realizing once again that the rich do have certain advantages: no fighting over limited access to beautiful views for one thing, immortality for another, or at least as long as their monuments endure. Vefa tells me one sultan had his entire harem sewn up in sacks and thrown in the Golden Horn. Did he watch from this window as his bagged concubines sank with a thousand sighs?

"Not every story has a happy ending."

"What is a happy ending, Vefa?"

"Not suffering too much."

KADIKÖY

When Vefa and I part ways, I am relieved to be free, even though striking out on my own and starting up conversations with men is tricky, and the women are even more guarded. Because I am staying in Kadıköy on the Asian side, there are fewer English speakers.

This is where I meet the stranger.

Our first encounter is on the last ferry from Eminonu to Kadıköy. Anxious to get home after a long day working in the markets and tourist restaurants in Sultanahmet, the Turks press together and surge to fill every available seat on the *feribot*.

They've earned their rest and I am a walking impropriety. That is obvious in the refusal of either men or women to smile back at the infidel with uncovered head and bare arms. Even the secular Turks appear to be shocked by the open, apparently guileless way I look into their eyes when I speak to them.

The stranger, however, looks up, and, putting his hand over his heart and bowing his head slightly, refuses to hear my insincere protests. I do want to sit down, and gladly take his seat as he stands for the twenty-minute passage across the Golden Horn, his legs braced against the rocking waves in waters rolling over drowned sailors and gold thrown into the channel to frustrate pillaging Ottoman soldiers.

I wonder if, when our eyes meet, he thinks he recognizes me from somewhere else. People my age have collected so many "might have beens." It is what we have. "*İnşallah,*" my stranger passes on a blessing. "*Teşekkurler,*" I respond as he steadies himself, grasping the rail. Twenty minutes later, the boat lands at the Kadıköy pier on the Asian side with a bump, and he vanishes into the crowds swarming around food vendors.

There is food for sale everywhere in Turkey: mussels and cobs of tough corn on the *feribot* wharves, and markets filled with fresh produce on every street. I am hungry, on my way to the Ciya Sofrası, a buffet-style restaurant in the fish market where Sweet Papa, who has been here before, brought us straight from the airport. To get there, I pass the fish stands and shops selling Turkish delight, spices and evil eyes for tourists.

I consider all the beautiful dishes laid out on the Ciya buffet and choose a plate of eggplant stuffed dolmas, a pomegranate and seaweed salad and, two desserts – glazed pumpkin and a bowl of fig and milk pudding that I know from my last visit will taste like my mother before she fell from grace.

Absorbed by my feast, I don't notice him until he interrupts. "*Merhaba.*"

I lower my sunglasses. *Feribotman* has found me at the sacred place where food is religion, every flavour balanced in God's kitchen. This is beyond coincidence.

Is he my deliverance or a carpet salesman looking for lonely women to seduce and fleece while the sun sets over the beautiful silhouettes of Sutanahmet, a phenomenon I've already assimilated in my chamber of souvenirs, a suite with a balcony overlooking the Bosphorus, my window on Istanbul despite the grime on the glass.

"*Merhaba*," I answer, impaling a piece of glazed pumpkin in walnut sauce on my fork, and then, after touching his heart again, he dissolves into the crowd like sugar in tea. My mutable stranger is gone. Never mind, I have a city to embrace.

Lemons. The next time, a day later, I smell him before I see him. "*Bozuk*," my recurring dream, standing beside me in front of a painting of two children riding a Turkish carpet at Sukran Sahin's art show at the Tünel Sanat Galerisi in old Istanbul, speaks again.

"*Bozuk*."

I feel his tartar vitality, his coiled intelligence. I smell the wind moving through lemon groves. Turning slightly, I see he is just a little taller than I am. His head is shaved.

"Broken," he translates.

"What?" I am confused.

"The dreams of children."

I hear the sound of belly dancers with coins sewn in their skirts and headdresses. I hear change falling from hand to hand in the Grand Bazaar. The Turks call their coins "*bozuk para.*"

"How?" I ask, and the stranger, who tells me his name is Güzel, sighs. He is going to tell me. Is my angel, Mr. Gudewill, smiling in heaven, his mission accomplished? And what about mine? After years of giving pleasure to others, I think I might find my own with this Turkish man who appears to be following me.

"We seem to be destined to meet. Would you like to have a glass of çay and talk about my country?" We walk out of the gallery onto the busy Istiklal Cadessi, and he leans a little closer because the noise of the vendors, pedestrians and the clattering trolley car make conversation almost impossible. We duck into one of the side streets in the flower market, where it is less noisy.

"I do have a question," I say, keeping up with his confident strides by dance-walking over the treacherous cobblestones and pavement cracks. If I try to stay in the air, I might not stumble. I would like to take his arm, but he hasn't offered it.

Since I am asking everyone I meet, "Why do Turks dislike Pamuk?" I go for the question. Mr. Gudewill would approve of a literary opening.

"Perhaps, after I have explained about my country, you will know."

"Perhaps?"

He doesn't answer. *İnşallah*, I keep up as he makes his way through the crowd.

"Good girl," Mr. Gudewill says.

At night, lying on my defiled mattress, I've been reading Pamuk's new novel, *The Museum of Innocence*, which is actually the story of this city. The narrator has been collecting memorabilia from his impossible love. In real life, Pamuk has been teasing his fans and detractors with an alleged museum of his own, also in Beyoğlu. Reportedly, he is filling it with ordinary things from his life and times. I imagine my stranger turning the pages for me, as if the book were music. Mr. Gudewill did that; anxious for me to read the passages he loved. "Ah, this is a good part."

My own personal tourist museum can't be any less fascinating than Pamuk's collection. My rooms at the Eysan Otel are littered with indiscreet evidence of quick carnal exchange between lonely men and women: empty condom wrappers and soiled underpants under the bed, stains on the mattress and post-coital cigarette burns on the blankets.

"Interesting," I said to my invisible bed partner last night, a new habit.

"Maybe I should be saving all these things. I could take them to Pamuk's *Museum of Innocence* and add them to his collection."

"We need artifacts," Pamuk wrote in his novel, which I have dog-eared shamelessly, "to better understand the lives of others, and our own."

Mr. Gudewill did not approve of turning down pages or underlining favourite passages. He said it was a desecration. I wondered if he were thinking of re-sale, if there might be bookstores in heaven; or if heaven is just a big museum like the undressing rooms in death camps, a place for storing our phenomenal lives before our souls are released?

I haven't saved the cigarette butts or false teeth of people I have loved, but, thanks to my father, I do have their fugitive voices captured in bottles.

"Here we are." Güzel orders tea and adds two lumps of sugar as soon as it arrives

"Pamuk's characters," he interrupts my thoughts, "are like insects trapped in tree sap, the slow moving streets of this beautiful city. Our old sidewalks crowded with vendors of fresh fruit, vegetables and fish, Ottoman princes, the descendants of families that have forgotten how to be useful in the world, refugees from the impoverished east crowding to the Promised

Land on the European boundary, and deranged soccer fans are a navigational nightmare.

"Only monuments like the Galata Tower, Attester and Galata Bridges and the architectural wonders of Sultanahmet, the Aya Sophia, the Topkapı Palace and the Blue Mosque help us navigate. Only the *feribots* crossing the waters leave and arrive on time. No one seems to know whether they are coming or going and they don't like our Nobel Prize-winning author drawing attention to this very fragile and deranged beehive." He barely takes a breath.

I wonder if I should kiss him.

"This city is all contradictions," he says. "If you've a date in Constantinople," the song says, "she'll be waiting in Istanbul."

I remember something Vefa said about Ozymandian melancholy. That could apply just as well to Istanbul as it does to Rome: Osmanli melancholy, beautiful women aging in gilded mirrors, the march of time. My new friends all seem so sad.

Güzel continues, "Young Turks, fearing jihad, erosion of democracy and the relentless grind of bottom feeding, confess they want to get out. Istanbul has changed. The exodus from the eastern provinces is choking our jewel of Byzantium. There are too many people and not enough room. No one can move. '*Göte giren şemsiye açılmaz,*' they say. "How can you open an umbrella if it is up your ass?"

He smiles and places his hands on the table. He is done.

"That's quite a speech. Are you a politician or a professor? Do you approach complete strangers in order to rehearse this lecture on Turkish culture?" I smile because I don't want to frighten him. I don't want his hand to move away from the table, where I can admire it. It is a small hand, smooth, beautifully made. He has not done manual work.

"Every tourist who comes to Istanbul wants to discuss politics and or Pamuk. We all have our answers ready." He laughs.

"I'll try to think of some new ones."

I get it. I ran into Doug, Sweet Papa Lowdown's sax player, who's been hanging out in the streets, reading comics and learning the language. He's calling their random tour the *Bozuk Iptal Umbrella Tour*, *iptal* meaning cancelled. Is this the world of Orhan Pamuk, a phenomenal mystery set in ruin and beauty, the remains of occupation and imperial glory where East met West and everyone got lost?

"Pamuk is one of the privileged. He grew up in a house that bears the name of his ancestors. His is the legacy of Byzantine anachronism, which is as often as not the prerogative to be and do nothing, to wait like an old beauty for the elixir of love to revivify her moldering body."

Güzel carries on talking but my mind wanders to my other agenda, Iman, who was betrayed by strangers. I want to bring up her name but am afraid to interrupt. Would that insult Turkishness?

When the world first saw Iman in the hotel in Tripoli, her headscarf had fallen off, her face was bruised, her eyes and lips swollen from crying. She showed us the rope burns on her wrists. There were other wounds but before we could see them a soldier disguised as a waitress had thrown her coat over her head. Then Iman was led out to a police car by Gaddafi goons and driven to God knows what horrible destination. What were her parents thinking as they watched helplessly on the other side of the revolutionary war? I can't imagine.

Will this stranger help? Dare I ask?

Later might be better. The band is playing at the Jazz Company near Taksim Square this evening. After a few *rakıs*, who knows?

"Would you like to hear my new friends play music to-night?"

"I have to work, but perhaps later."

"Do you know the Jazz Company?"

"Of course. I will try to be there."

I love the evening walks down Istiklal: the ice cream clowns, the cafés, the music, the fairy lights dancing over the street and, of course, the people. By the time I cross Taksim Square, it is dark and the political speakers of the day are gone, replaced by vendors selling stuffed mussels and corn and girls wearing light-up Minnie Mouse bows in their hair.

The Jazz Company, a club in a Western-style hotel only a block from the square, is another world. It could be upscale anywhere. The band is just setting up and there are only a few businessmen and their girlfriends drinking at the chic bar. Güzel has not yet arrived. Not wanting to appear anxious, I was hoping to arrive after him. I do not like sitting in bars by myself, but here I am, trying not to stare at the demonstrably primed couple at the next table.

Cagdas, the Sweet Papa Lowdown Turkish drummer, pulls up a chair and orders a *raki* and *mezzes* for me. "I get it free with the gig."

"Aren't you hungry? Aren't you thirsty? "

"I don't drink and I won't have time to eat, so enjoy it for me."

I wonder if he is telling me the truth. There is no end to the hospitality of Turks.

"Check out our neighbours," I say.

The man is sipping champagne and passing it by mouth to his partner. They look European, possibly German, but speak Turkish. Everything is unpredictable in Turkey, except for the women in *hajibs*, but maybe not them either. I remember stories of Muslim women on wild shopping sprees in the lingerie department at Harrods in London. This woman could be in her underwear; she is that indiscreet. She puts her tongue in his ear.

"That's enough for me," Cagdas says, " I gotta play."

As the club fills up and the band starts playing, my neighbours turn up the volume. Having given up on Güzel, I pass the time by trying to understand their conversation, which is turning belligerent. Their exchange sounds as feral as the cats that fight and fuck in the street outside my hotel. His fingers circle her wrist like a handcuff. She spits in his face. This is the tipping point. He stands up.

"*Orospu!*" he screams, 'slut,' picks up his chair and, barely missing her, smashes it down on the glass tabletop, and then stalks out of the club.

The band carries on, perhaps a bit faster, "*When the sun goes down in Harlem*," Jeff sings, and the woman stays seated, her face inscrutable.

"Do you speak English?" I lean over and ask.

She gets up, brushes away the slivers of glass as if they were pollen. "Yes, but I must leave."

"He might have killed you." By now, several waiters are sweeping up the glass and removing the broken chair.

"He is my husband," she says, shrugging, as if this behaviour were marital foreplay.

"Men like that don't know when to stop," I insist. " One day he will kill you."

She says nothing but keeps looking at the door, as if he might come back. "Excuse me. I have to go to the washroom."

I watch her speak to a waiter and hand him money. Then she leaves. I follow as far as the door. Her husband is waiting on the street and they walk off toward the crowds in Taksim Square, arm in arm, vanishing in the night to an ending I don't want to imagine.

Is this secularism for Turkish women, who can show their faces and drink and still be abused?

"Is there something I don't understand?" I ask the waiter. "What just happened?"

"She paid for the drinks and she paid for the damage, fifteen hundred lira." He shrugs.

"Not a good one," Güzel says later, when I tell him the story.

"What did you say?"

CHRISTMAS

At night, festive strings of lights illuminate the Istaklal Cadessi. Even in May, it feels like Christmas. I close my eyes and smell snow, remembering a moment with my parents. Was it an acrobatic trick or grace, the two of them balanced on the curb waiting for a light to change the day of the Santa Claus parade? They were not touching, each of them together, each of them alone, outlined in light, with the pale winter sun in front of them. The day was cold. I watched our breath condense. I was four years old, standing in their shadows.

My mother and father, I thought, were unassailable, divine. I could not see my father's imperfect heart beneath his impeccably tailored overcoat. He kept at a safe distance from my mother and her insatiable hunger for love. I could see the cold space between them.

Years later, waiting for a stoplight to turn green at an intersection in the Kootenay Mountains, I looked up and saw a thunderhead shaped like an angel. The big black cloud was etched in light the colour of precious metal, the gilded surrounds of medieval religious paintings. By then, both my parents had gone to Heaven or whatever follows this sprint over broken glass.

My memories of those moments are soundless. Is unheard music the necessary matrix of human relationships? Have I been creating a jigsaw of human shapes circumscribed by blinding light? A holy family, is that the incandescence Pamuk sensed when he said he heard God in the silence of snow? I have felt this; but I need a guide to lead me to an understanding of my own feelings.

After the Christmas I witnessed the miracle of the curb, my father took me to visit the parents of friends who had been killed in the last war. I was the future, what their boys had died for. Was I a compensatory angel there to remind them that their sons had not been sacrificed in vain? Now this notion disturbs me, but at the time I understood his need to spoon my future into their hungry void. I could see the bereaved parents turning from my father's anxious offertory.

Feeling their exacerbated unhappiness, my father began singing desperately, the way his own father had on one famous truce in the trenches of World War One – "Silent Night," the words heavy with meaning. That silence was death. The guns began firing immediately afterward. My grandfather was gassed. His friend lost an eye.

Grief, the loneliness of the survivor, slowly killed my father. I am sure that every sip of forgetfulness was self-medication for the sickness of knowing that his young friends had died for no reason. How many Jews did they save? How many gypsies? What sort of peace did the U.N. peacemakers leave in Korea? How many child soldiers have been brought to redemption by "peaceful" intervention in Afghanistan, Sierra Leone, Darfur, Rwanda, or Angola? How many Palestinian or Afghani infants will have milk and medicine because other children have been convinced to blow themselves up in public places? Not enough. Never enough.

My father and the men and women who have followed him into subsequent battlefields appear to have saved the world for condos, cappuccinos, and jets that tear much larger holes in the ozone than the needle-eyed cracks angels pass through. They are all damaged. When my mother took me to visit him in the hospital, I saw in his eyes, as large and innocent as at the moment of his birth, the knowledge of finite space. That knowledge could not be drowned in whiskey or the hunger of women who may have picked his pocket while they pleasured him. It can only be redeemed by love as brilliant as miracles.

I became a creator of miracles as soon as I could speak. Even today I cannot tell the difference between my real memory and magical thinking. Did I imagine all the good news to comfort myself, or the people who live without hope? My mother used to say she knew when I was telling a lie, because I blinked. It is impossible to stare directly at the sun or at a lie. Was I lying to myself when I saw my parents standing at the light, waiting to go forward? They were not angels. I wonder how hard it is going to be for me to become one.

Is my stranger, Güzel, the perfect companion, the perfect angel who will understand whatever it is I am trying to find out?

SEVMEK

E-mail to the motherboard

In Turkish, my name is Güzel, which means "beautiful" or "lovely." We are all the mutable Sevmek, which is the verb "to love," perhaps a little too, as we say in English, "close" for my companion?

Like the first people from Madeleine's country, Turks choose real names for their children. A child born in the morning might be called Sunrise. A child born without pain might be called Grace. A child conceived in a farmer's field might be called Harvest. I have picked an active verb, the one that obsesses Madeleine, who has given and never received the love she needs and deserves. That, to my thinking, is most appropriate, as is the name of Iman, the young woman she wants to save through her caring.

Getting close is my vocation. For now, I am close to Mad. Proximity is my gift to her. She seems quite determined to find love in Turkey (is this an Iman projection?), and I am here to make sure she doesn't lose herself in the process.

She was named after the little French orphan in the story-book, the girl who had difficulty marching in two straight rows with her convent companions and ended up falling into the Seine. The shit disturber. I call her independent, resilient. Then she became Mother. How absurd is this reversal of roles? What an obscenity.

I will call Madeleine Mad in this diary because this is her season of madness, *sa saison enfer,* and that is a good thing. Madeleine, Mother, Mad is transposing herself. That in itself is a separate reality, her existential time.

For your information, I speak fluent Turkish. The truth is, I can love in any language. The short answer is, I do not intrude. I respond to invitation.

Madeleine sent a note, which incidentally, she signed "Mad," to Postsecrets, a website where people reveal their innermost thoughts on postcards. Some of the letters are comical and some profoundly touching. The site receives confessions to terrible crimes and perversions, but most messages admit to the pain of loneliness. Mad sent in a card on which she had drawn a big magnifying glass focused on a tiny red heart. Beside it she had written in a cartoon bubble, "Please find me." That was no problem. She was postmarked, "Istanbul." She has always been hungry but now she is ready; and so I found her crossing the Bosphorus to Ciya.

My tentative position requires browsing in places like Postsecrets to find clients. When I see that someone needs a friend, I will become that friend. The client may or may not be aware of my presence. Mad is a very intuitive person. I think she is responding to my energy. She's beginning to extrapolate my intervention into a presence in the phenomenal world, a real companion.

Let me introduce myself properly. I am a virtual companion, or at least I am apprenticing for that profession. Just as lawyers, doctors, goldsmiths, leather-smiths, printers and architects used to apprentice to masters, I am attached to a master, Sevmek. We are, in a sense, the long arms of Sevmek. Hopefully, before long, virtual companionship will be a reality and no one will need to be alone.

For now, I travel with the pioneer of fifth-dimensional friendship, both of us navigating on faith. We are in new territory, our old calling now assisted by social media. My master has been around since the first creature with a designed intelligence crawled out of the sea. My colleagues and I have been called angels, chimera, doppelgangers, what have you. We have hovered over mosques and churches and synagogues, listening to the troubled, healing the sick, protecting the besieged or careless and carrying off the dead.

I knew Mad when she was a kid. She had a little Electrolux vacuum cleaner savings bank. The bank held quarters. When it was full it popped open and the money came out. Mad would take her quarters to a payphone and call the North Pole. I visited her then. Spending a summer with her was my first job after rapturing. I loved it, and Madeleine was one of my favourite clients. When she turned up on Postsecrets decades later, I remembered her right away; and that is how I came to be in Turkey, one of the reasons.

This is a different world. Now our clients type and scroll, make commands instead of praying. I wouldn't go so far as to call this generation inspired but I would say they still deserve redemption. You may or may not realize that redemption happens one unit at a time. Because we have free will, it is not a sweeping universal thing. We have chosen to be alienated, to converse through machines, to think with machines, and to destroy with machines. This may not be a good thing, but we do have the opportunity to use the new mind control to our advantage. We can teach people to love and be loved. That is my job description in the social media.

My boss is no Luddite when it comes to technology. You might argue that science is the devil's work, a potential weapon of mass destruction, and I am tempted to agree. But don't forget the devil is a fallen angel, a very important angel, the angel of light.

When Madeleine was a little girl, she was obsessed with neon. That makes sense. Her father, whom I have accompanied on several transitions, was in the movie business. Little Madeleine would stand outside the Odeon Theatre, marvelling at the marquee. She thought her dad was Reddy Kilowatt, Master of the Electric Universe. Close, Mad, close. He understood the real import of moving pictures.

Then the lights went out. She's been groping in the dark for most of her life, looking for that tiny bulb that would give her hope, not realizing that it was in her all the time. My job is to help turn Madeleine on. She is ready. That will help her. The name Iman means faith. She knows what she is looking for in this earthquake zone we call Turkey.

APPLE TEA

I've learned two important things about tea. The first came from the Poet Laureate of England; those pesky metal teapots don't leak if you open the lid before pouring. If you are wondering how I met him, he was a client. And he stiffed me, but I was glad to discover the bit about teapots. That was worth a free hour on my table.

The second revelation was that adding cream eliminates the liver's nauseous response to drinking on an empty stomach. The Turks put sugar in their tea and that also avoids the bad reaction.

I gave the British Poet Laureate a special massage on one of his fishing trips to British Columbia. Later, when I asked him to sign my book at his reading, he ignored me. I have great sympathy for the invisibles of this life. I wonder if the literary world would be interested in knowing that the poet shouted his sister's name when he came in my hand?

My stranger's name is Güzel. I have already looked in my Turkish phrase book and confirmed that the word does indeed mean "beautiful."

"Did you just make this up, or am I imagining you?"

"Both," my enigmatic new friend smiles. I smile back because I have heard that showing teeth releases endorphins. My heart is behaving like a cat in heat, rolling all over my chest. The French say hunger is the best sauce and I am as ravenous as the cats that come to the Kadıköy *kitapçı* at teatime.

"What is your last name?" I ask, knowing I'll forget it right away because Turkish names are so different from ours.

"Melek."

"Which means?" Everything, I now know, has meaning in Turkey.

"Angel." He smiles.

"You're teasing me."

"Not at all. And I am going to give you flying lessons." He laughs.

Surprisingly, because I have introduced myself as Mad, maybe a joke, he knows my full name, Madeleine Turka. I don't suppose my parents ever thought I'd be shortened to "Mad Turk," but there it is. Here I am. When Güzel tells me it was Ataturk who insisted all of his countrymen take a surname, I realize it was the Italians who called my first Tuscan ancestor "Turka," the Turk.

"Touristic restaurants charge several times as much as Turkish," he says on the short walk to the old flower-selling district, taking my elbow and steering me past cafés with menus in English and Turkish in the windows and the Starbucks near the gallery on İstiklal Caddesi. I ask him to walk slowly because my calves are screaming. Once again I am stiff and lurching like a toddler with pleated thighs after climbing the Galata Hill to Beyoğlu yesterday.

"You should take the *Tünel*," he laughs, explaining about the train that carries passengers up and down the hill for a cost of less than one lira. I don't tell him that I know about the train but believe walking up hills is good for my figure.

Now we are sitting in a small restaurant with benches covered with carpets in the Cicek Pasajı, known as the Flower Passage. I am stirring my *çay* with a small spoon and having a histamine reaction to Güzel's chocolate-brown eyes, an addiction that must be in my DNA. If I look into them, my knees will melt and I won't be able to get up and leave if, or when, he makes a lunge for my purse or my bosom. Isn't that a contradiction? Didn't I just think that I was willing to take off my clothes and jump right into those muddy pools? Welcome to my world of contradictions!

"Here, the *çay* is one lira. You'd pay five in those other places."

"In Victoria we all pay tourist prices."

"Victoria is an English name."

"We were a colony." The absurdity has just struck me, the endangered lives of bees.

"Turks don't care much for the English." Güzel looks away for the first time.

"They brought pederast clergymen and smallpox to Canada."

"Smallpox? We have a British smallpox story too. Who do you suppose invented the cure?"

"Wasn't it Jenner?"

"No, it was Turkish dairymen who discovered their workers were immune. The wife of the British ambassador to Turkey, Lady Montagu, her own beauty stolen by the disease, had her son inoculated and took the discovery back to

England. You English have a long history of stealing ideas and antiquities."

"I'm not English and not American. I'm Canadian." I don't tell him that my father might have been Turkish. What if it isn't true? What if my father's family had been English ex-pats taking a fanciful name and living the good life at the end of the Silk Road, promenading on the backs of ordinary Turks? I just took my mother's word for this provenance. There is little documentation for either side of the family, no scrapbooks or home movies. My mother was not sentimental that way, but she was intuitive.

"Do you dislike tourists?" he asks.

"We co-exist. Many people make their living from tourism."

"We are business people too."

"The customer is always right," I say, repeating the only proverb to come out of our capitalist society; and he shakes his head from side to side, which, in Turkey, means agreement. The problem is that tourists and customers can turn into colonizers. It is safer to be wary.

"What business are you in?"

"I'm a Hell's Angel," I answer.

"What does that mean? You ride a motorcycle?"

"No," I laugh too loudly, and men in the café turn to look at us, a Turkish man and a Canadian woman. "I escort old ladies and gentlemen to the gates of Paradise."

"You said Hell."

"You can never be too sure what might be waiting on the other side of a door or who might be turned away, can you?"

"When you have been in Turkey for a while you will really know the meaning of that."

I think I already do. The polite honking that characterizes Istanbul's anarchistic traffic could be a dissembling metaphor for this diverse culture. The gun shops in the Galata tunnel are the other side of that conceit.

"Perhaps it will be easier for me because I am used to living in the moment. I take care of the elderly, a sort of companion and practical nurse." I smile when I say that because the practicality includes sexual services. I wonder if Güzel would be shocked if I were to tell him straight out.

" I give hand releases to my patients." There. There it is, and he hardly reacts. "It relaxes them. They sleep better when they are happy."

"And you?"

"I sleep well."

"No, I mean, does your work make you happy?"

"Yes. I think of it as a vocation, strange as that sounds."

"You mean a holy vocation?"

"Well yes, I guess it could be. I call it kindness."

"You do have a kind face," he says. His, I notice, is closed. His expression, or non-expression, is resolute, passionate but inscrutable. A dark viscosity in his eyes and appetite in his full mouth and strong white teeth. His face is hungry but guarded.

"I am kind. We are culturally kind, overly polite, just like the Turks."

"Sometimes we are too kind."

"Personally or politically?"

"Kindness is a good thing until someone takes advantage. Sometimes a man will take advantage of a kind woman. The same thing happens between religions and countries. In the belief that they are acting out of kindness, doing the right thing, people can behave very badly."

"Idealism is the mother of arrogance."

"The Americans are a good example with their exportation of 'freedom.'"

"What about the deep history here?" I realize that is a hostile question, but I ask it anyway because Güzel makes me feel careless enough to make the jump with him from sex to politics. "What about the Armenian Massacre?" I press.

"That was before Ataturk."

"Everything starts with Ataturk then?"

"Modern Turkey starts with Kemal. Whatever happened in the past is past. Isn't it better for us to focus on living in peace in the present?"

"What about admitting accountability and then moving on?"

"That's just it. Not everyone would agree. There would be arguments about how many died, and there would be arguments about reparations. We would have to bring up Armenian conspiracy with the Russians. The Russians, by the way, are not our friends. That discussion would never end and what would it solve? It wouldn't change the past. We have real problems to solve in the present. That is what we should be thinking about."

Since we are experiencing the scorching evidence of global warming and potential fallout from the Arab Spring, I have to agree with him.

The Turkish election will take place a few days after I leave at the end of May. Güzel tells me that the streets of every town along the Sea of Marmara to the Aegean and the Mediterranean, from Istanbul to Bodrum, are festooned with red banners bearing the image of the long dead Father of Turkey, just like Istanbul, which could be a ship coming into port with all its flags flying. Güzel says Ataturk rises from his grave every time it is necessary to protect his vision of a secular and inclusive nation. Now as before, the past wants to swallow the present.

"Like Canada, we are a compromise, not a solution."

"You seem to know a lot about politics."

"It is my job."

"I'm sorry. I didn't ask. What do you do?" I lean forward.

"I am a journalist."

"Ahhh!" I say.

I had assumed he was a tourist walker or a government agent.

"What do you mean, 'Ahhh?'"

"I thought perhaps you'd been sent to me for a different reason. You are interviewing me. What does a foreigner make of the Turkish situation? I thought you found me attractive."

"I do. You are a beautiful woman. I am also curious. What do you think of Turkey?"

"That's good. Do you really want to hear what I think?" I read, it might have been in the Eyewitness guidebook, that there are several cardinal rules for tourist behaviour in Turkey. Dress modestly. Do not demean the memory of Ataturk. Do not blow your nose in public or put your feet on a table, however low. Do not go barefoot. Do not criticize Turkish customs.

The Turkish lamb has teeth. It is in reality Aslan, the lion. The Turks, like the Syrians simmering next door, are a pluralistic society.

"I think that in some ways Turkey is like Canada. Our countries are misunderstood by the world at large because they have no idea of our national character."

"Why is that?"

"That is because we don't tell them."

"Do you think a country should have secrets?" He smiles. I think Güzel smiles whenever the questions are hard. That might give him time to experience an endorphin rush and defuse his irritation.

"How would we know if it did or it didn't? No one tells the truth."

"How can you be sure?"

"Because it is my job to find it."

When I told people that I was coming to Turkey, they warned me about Byzantine politics and microbes. They said I would be lucky to leave with my life. The television news back home showed violent demonstrations in Ankara. All I have seen relating to the election in Istanbul are flags and trucks with recorded messages and rap songs urging the Turks to get out and vote for their candidates.

We are drowned out. A distraction has appeared in the form of a large family accompanied by musicians, all dancing attendance on a pre-adolescent boy dressed in a strangely comic military uniform, like a majorette's, with a red satin cape and gold hat. The boy looks nervous as the family members take up several outdoor tables, which the waiters quickly cover with *mezzes:* olives, tomatoes, cucumber, cheese, bread, yogurt, and dolmades.

"Is it his birthday? He doesn't look all that thrilled." I ask.

"They are celebrating his *Kitan*, or circumcision." I notice the word is close to *kitap*, for book, and *kirtan*, the Sikh dagger.

"Poor little thing. Is his book opening or closing?"

"Both. It's a proud and painful day for him. He is a man. Manhood does not come easily."

"Nor does womanhood," I add, watching the female relatives sweating in their shrouds.

We stay quiet while the guests attach gold coins to the boy's costume and others dance in the street. His table piles high with gifts. Today, clearly, he is a little prince, albeit one with sore genitals. I want to ask if they also circumcise the girls, but this time discretion banishes boldness and we observe, sipping our tea.

"Would it be rude if I took his picture?" I whisper to Güzel, even though I already know it is rare for a Turk to refuse any request

"You could ask," is his enigmatic answer.

The parents say yes and I shoot the little boy from above, the giant's perspective. Do we all look so large to him that he dare not protest or is he comforted by all the bigness that surrounds him? Surely the adults will take care of him, even on this day, his first step to adulthood.

When I check the photograph, I see a brave smile and fear in his eyes. Poor child, poor country, teetering between realities, past and present, East and West.

At another table a man is feeding bits of meat to a small bird cradled in his hand. I am surprised by his tenderness. When I catch his eye, he smiles. When I raise my camera again, he looks away. I understand. I hate to pose. That's why I am the one taking the pictures.

When Güzel and I finish our second glass of tea, I insist on paying the waiter. I am going to concede to laziness and hop on the *Tünel* streetcar that will take me down a steep tunnel to the Galata Bridge.

"How far is the fish market from the end of the bridge?"

"Five hundred metres," he answers without hesitating, pointing to the left. "Did you know that the game was named after our bridge? The British soldiers crossed it from their barracks to play a new game on the other side. They called it 'bridge.'"

"I don't play," I say, pinching myself. That is a lie. I play whist, abbreviated bridge, with my clients. The brain exercise helps to keep them mentally agile. I don't want to end up playing card games and giving hand releases to beautiful Turkish men, especially not this one. Bridge is work, and I am not here to work.

"Next time we will have apple tea." Güzel opens the door and I think he is saying apple "tree" because my hearing is deteriorating, something I attribute to shouting at old men who are too vain to wear their hearing aids.

I do hear the song my mother sang when she was four sheets to the wind, *Don't sit under the apple tree with anyone else but me.* Was she afraid my father would transgress in heaven before she got there? She sang it as if her heart was breaking and I spun until I was dizzy on the kitchen floor. Was this how it felt to be drunk? If she saw me fall over, would she stop and pick me up? I saw little lights flitting in front of my face. Were they fireflies or angels?

"Why *did* you come to my country, a woman alone?" Güzel asks, instead of shaking my hand when we part on the street. I had been wondering if he would take my offered hand or kiss me on both cheeks. There is unfinished business.

"Ah," I pause. "I came to find a reporter who would get the government's attention."

"Why would you want to do that?" he smiles.

"Because someone is lost."

"We are all lost, Madeleine."

"This is important."

"It's always important."

"Do you know about Iman al-Obeidi?"

"Of course. Why do you ask?"

" I ask because every other Turk I've run into has no idea who I am talking about and someone has to help her."

"I think a lot of people are trying. You know about the online petition?"

"Of course, and I'm asking you to help make sure Erdoğan takes it seriously."

" I am just one small man and there is more than one side to Erdoğan. The Kemalists are waiting for the other shoe to drop and you can be sure it will."

"But you have a voice."

"Is that why you found me?"

"I thought it was the other way round."

Just as Güzel disappears into the crowd, my blues band entourage waves to me from the Olympiat restaurant on the fish wharf at Karakoy and I wander over. They are having *mezzes* and drinking foamy *ayran* from beaten copper cups with brass handles and glasses of *çay*.

"No *rakı* this afternoon? " I ask. "Too early," Naomi replies. She's been busy charming a pair of *rakı* salt and peppershakers out of a waiter who has the conflicted expression all Turkish boys take on the moment they meet her. I wonder what they think of the *yabancı piliç* with her direct gaze and short skirts? She is so different from the Turkish girls, so in charge of her sensuality, which she wears like a beautiful mask as impervious as a *hajib*.

"Where are Kris and Doug?" I ask.

"They're recording at Baykuş Studio."

A woman who looks like Iman walks by, and I almost jump out of my chair.

"Someone you know?" Hannah, the observant one, asks.

"No, I keep seeing people who look like Iman al-Obeidi."

Rick, who must think I need distraction, pulls a plastic bag out of his pocket. "I stole this from the Blue Mosque. It's a shoe bag, sacred Turkish comb plastic." Sweet Papa Lowdown is a band of magpies. "Have you been yet?"

"No but I will, but I won't be stealing anything. How are you going to explain all this weird stuff you're collecting when you go through customs?"

"We'll quote Pamuk,." Hannah the Reader looks up from my dog-eared copy of *The Museum of Innocence*, "...to better understand the lives of others and our own."

We are quiet, even Naomi and Hannah, even though they don't yet know all that we know. We all carry memories as heavy as stones on our wings, the past weighing on all of us, as it does on this ancient city.

CANADA

I must have a scarlet letter on my forehead – " C" for Canada, or a red maple leaf. Wherever I go in Istanbul, people follow me in the street, asking if I am Canadian. How else would they know? I see clothes very much like the ones I wear in the markets here. I run into blond tourists speaking Dutch and German. I don't see many black people. How strange with Africa so close.

"One hundred and eighty-nine."

"What?" I haven't told Güzel about the game.

"I have counted one hundred and eighty-nine persons of colour."

"We are all persons of colour, Madeleine," he replies, quite rightly.

"No, I mean Black People."

"Why would you do such a thing? It sounds like the American red and orange alerts, what we call 'the rainbow of fear.'"

"Who is we?"

"Us."

"*Comment?*" I can't think of an English word that fits better.

"My people."

"Ah, well, the son one of my clients, who is a Black Person, noticed that he was singular in Istanbul. Everyone thought he was Barack Obama."

"Sweet," my enigmatic companion offers.

"I'm counting and will report back to him. The funny thing is I met Christina, a Canadian non-profit worker, while listening to music at the Polka Café in Moda this afternoon. She's counting too."

"What will your friend think of you and your white sister standing on street corners counting Black People?"

"I am not standing on street corners. I am moving about, minding my business."

"You think Turks are racist?"

"No, I am just trying to figure out why a country so close to Africa has no Africans, apart from tourists."

"Why would they come where there are no jobs? Besides, it was the son of an American slave who brought jazz to Istanbul. They called him the Sultan of Jazz."

"One person isn't exactly a diaspora."

"Don't forget the eunuchs."

"Ah, so the word is out. Every man who fails the comb and brown paper bag tests at the Istanbul airport gets his balls chopped off?" And, just in case he doesn't understand the American roots reference, I explain. "Blacks couldn't get into certain clubs and juke joints if their hair didn't pass through ordinary combs and their skin was darker than brown paper bags."

"We are not responsible for the paranoid imaginings of tourists."

There is no getting around Güzel. He has already thought of everything.

Tonight I have invited him to a violin and piano concert at the Moda Opera House, a modified-baroque post-Ataturk building blending the Turkish fascination with European decoration and the clean lines of the secular regime. The hall, its boxes hung with red velvet draperies and gold details, brings to mind the sequined evening gowns hanging in cheap dress shops in the markets. I wonder if these garments are worn by Turkish ladies or the Russian prostitutes that obsess Berk, the Sweet Papa Lowdown slide guitarist, who says whole towns along the Black Sea in this sexually repressed country have been bankrupted by the introduction of expensive Ukrainian hookers. People trafficking through Istanbul is no secret. I can't imagine what will happen when the dam busts and the Middle East pours into Turkey.

Tonight the program is European, a sonata by Grieg and a Beethoven concerto. We were almost late. A shoeshine man on the street dropped his brush while apparently running for a dolmuş. When I picked it up and ran after him, he offered to shine my shoes. Realizing that he wanted to thank me, I didn't want to insult him by refusing or offering a tip and yet, when I thanked him and started to walk away, he came after me asking for ten lira.

"What should I do?" I asked Güzel.

"It's a scam," he answered. "Do what you like."

"Why didn't you warn me?"

"You wouldn't have believed me."

What a strange country. Every experience is a parable. What odd people, so civil and yet so obtuse. I gave the shoeshine man five lira.

Berk, the slide guitarist, waves to me in the lobby. I notice he is wearing earplugs. When I mime the question, why, he shrugs. I notice he still has them on when he sits down three rows in front of us. How odd, I think, a musician wearing earplugs at a concert.

My jaw drops when the musicians appear on stage with their page turner. The pianist, a beauty, whose voluptuous face could fit the cherubs painted on the ceiling as easily as portraits of odalisques, is the very image of Iman. I rub my eyes, grope in my purse for my glasses. Surely not. Or, I rationalize, perhaps she is one of the Mediterranean stereotypes, a face as ubiquitous as olives.

"What's wrong?" The voice in the dark is concerned.

This time I whisper, "I keep seeing her."

"Don't worry," he says. "I hear that Iman is safe in Qatar."

"Safe," I repeat to myself as I sit back in my seat and enjoy the exquisite dialogue between the violin and piano in Beethoven's second movement. The pianist has beautiful dynamics and a tone as rich as her velvet dress.

"How do you know," I ask later, over a cup of foamy *ayran* at the Polka Café.

"It's still a secret. You haven't been hearing anything because she's still in danger."

"Evil has no political boundaries. Does this mean you won't be writing about her?"

"It wouldn't be wise."

"What about the petition to President Erdoğan?"

"That has been delivered, but you won't hear any more about it. Not for the time being."

Voltaire said redemption was possible if we just cultivated our gardens. I am not so sure. In Turkey, I understand that gardening is practical, its bounty found in the markets filled with spices, tomatoes, cucumbers, figs, olives, and artichokes. In Victoria where I live, the cultivation of plants is competitive. Who can grow the biggest dahlias, the most exotic roses? Who can name every variety of lilies? English settlers brought their snobbery with their oak trees. Even the gardens, passed down now, have a hierarchy, a detail that hasn't gone unnoticed by the Songhees People. "What is the point of growing grass," asked an aboriginal friend, who was admiring the spirit tree in my rubble heap when I apologized for the state of my yard, "if you can't eat it?"

What is so Canadian about me? Do I have green thumbs? Do I have a built-in personal ozonator? Do I smell like snow? Will having a colder climate spare us when climate change dries up equatorial gardens?

In Auschwitz, where I understand the Germans had exquisite gardens maintained by the prisoners, Canada was the shed where inmates checked their belongings. I've seen photos of that Canada, the piles of shoes and family silver, and the workers who were allowed to grow their hair after being shaved and de-loused.

As I walk past the hotels and street cafés in Beyoğlu and Sultanahmet, I wonder where the Hungarian Jew, Joseph Brandt, braced himself with a cup of Turkish coffee for the negotiation that could have saved the lives of a million Hungarian Jews? Did that coffee churn in his stomach and back up, burning his anxious throat as he groped for the words he would need to barter so many human souls for trucks for the Third Reich? Did he look over to the Asian side, hoping relief for his people would come from the Holy Land? When his desperate diplomacy failed, did he consider throwing himself into the Bosphorus, where long ago the Byzantines chucked their household valuables to avoid giving them up to the Ottomans?

"Canada" was the death camp equivalent to the treasure-filled channel that is the Golden Horn, a place where personal belongings were forfeited with no chance of getting them back. I always thought the inmates of Auschwitz called that shop of horrors after my country because the building wasn't heated. Mr. Gudewill told me of a Canada capo, one of the Jewish trusties with lighter jobs, who risked her life to secure a heater for a handful of new mothers and babies who had somehow survived pregnancy in the death camp. One of those mothers is still alive. She emigrated to Canada and ran a Judaica shop he had visited in Toronto.

"Good one," I said, and he looked startled.

The equation of my country with Arctic conditions is not exclusive to Americans. There were many delusional misconceptions among the starving population at the concentration camps. Newcomers wanted to believe the ashes falling from the crematorium chimneys were snow.

Recently, I read that the conventional wisdom was that Canada was abundant, a new Eden, the Promised Land. The inmate workers in Canada had certain privileges. They might find a piece of bread or chocolate in the pocket of an abandoned coat while they were sorting clothes. Paradise. Never mind that we are squandering that blessing, our water and our wilderness, in the spirit of competition, the bad seeds that were planted by the first settlers. Still, it is paradise, which I was told means an enclosed garden in Farsi, compared to what? Isn't everything about perception? No wonder our Aboriginal people admire the shape-changing Raven. Does Raven have limitless points of view? I know he brings the light. Is that the real matrix of tolerance? Am I going to learn how to be like a raven in this polyglot society? Did I come here for flying lessons as my stranger has intuited?

CHOCOLATE SUNDAY

One hot evening in my eleventh summer, I caught Coon stealing transparent apples from our tree. While lying on the lawn cart on the deck counting stars way past midnight, I heard a loud crack. Years later, I heard the same sound when an orthopedic surgeon snapped the adhesions I'd developed in my shoulder from diminishing lubricants and all the body work I've done. That time, the noise was a branch breaking.

Because his eyes shone in the leaves, I thought at first that the intruder was a raccoon. I wasn't scared of him. Faster than cotton candy dissolves in your mouth, I was off the deck and halfway up the apple tree.

I have a thing for raccoons. Once, I brought a whole family of orphans in the house and fed them with an eyedropper. When they no longer drank from a baby bottle with a rubber nipple, I set them free in the bushes – all but Bandit who had learned to pee in the toilet. He was my friend until he too, of course, ran away.

Coon was no four-legged highwayman, just a dirty boy looking for food. I called my wild boy "Coon" because as far as

I knew he didn't have a name. Besides, he was just like a raccoon: cute, sometimes vicious, and a wicked scavenger. The only difference was that raccoons travel with their tribe. My Coon was all by himself, with no one to help him or hold him down.

I didn't know any of that the first time I spotted him up in the branches filling his face and his pockets with the green cooking apples Stella made into apple pie, apple cobbler, apple sauce and apple butter back in the good old days when my dad was alive and she was a real mother.

At first I thought Coon was just some neighborhood brat spying on us or taking a dare. Most of the kids had heard Stella was crazy and there were rumours she had a shotgun and would blow the arse end off anyone making a getaway through the loose boards in our fence. That was bull tweedy. There *were* guns in our house but my mother wouldn't have known the goodbye end from the trigger. They were my father's war souvenirs.

I heard some of the neighbourhood boys had tomboy tests, and if the girls wanted to get into the boys' forts they had to pass dares, like swinging over the ravine on a rope and stealing stuff from our yard. Half of our yard burglars wet themselves because they were afraid my mother was going to haul herself off her Easyboy and blow their heads off when she heard them rummaging through the piles of household junk, my father's memorabilia from the Italian and Korean campaigns, and tools rusting in the back forty.

Coon didn't budge out of that tree. He just sat there. I climbed up.

"That's stealing, you know." I pushed my face close. "This is *my* tree."

Coon admitted nothing, but up close his breath smelled of apples. As soon as you look at transparent cooking apples, they start to bruise. Coon shrugged and went back to stuffing them in his pie hole as fast as they would fit. I gave up, picked one for myself and ate it too. So that was it; just the two of us sitting on separate branches in the moonlight eating and watching the car lights flicker and fade as, just like horses that know their way back to the barn, they drove themselves and the drunks behind the wheels home to bed. It was very quiet. All we could hear was chewing and swallowing and cat fights down the lane. Inside the house, Stella's late-night movie cast its grey pall over the living room, leaking through cracks in the curtains while she drank gin out of one of her goddamned china teacups.

"Cat got your tongue?" I asked. Then, when that didn't get a response, "You're lucky our dog is asleep." Frend was getting pretty old by then. He slept twenty-three hours a day and only woke up for his chip steak sandwiches and trips to his toilet, the yard next door, where I had to go with a poop shovel and pick his love droppings off the lawn every day after school so Mr. and Mrs. Fussypants wouldn't call the pound to come after him. Coon just ignored me. He picked himself a few more apples, packed them in his pockets, then slid down the tree and over the back fence. He was gone.

That was it, no more wild boy. I spent the rest of that summer looking for him. First off, I drew a sketch with WANTED FOR STEALING APPLES written over the top and put it in the Jung's grocery store. Nobody knew about Coon. The only inquiries I got were phone calls from kids wanting to know about the reward. Everyone in town seemed to know about the boxes of gratis complaint candy I got for writing letters about weight scams and low nut counts that I had stashed in the attic.

That gave me an idea. Back when we were still a family, my father read fairy tales while I sat on the floor next to the big velour chair in the living room and my mother washed the dinner dishes. In those days nobody but him got to sit in the Easyboy, ever. Then it became Stella's. After his final curtain, his widow nuzzled up to his chair like it was Daddy himself. Sometimes I caught her sniffing the headrest for traces of his hair oil or riding the arm like a deranged cowgirl.

I liked his hair oil and tobacco smells too. His fingers smelled of cigarettes and popcorn. I picked up the scent when he turned the pages in my storybooks. Then I closed my eyes and pretended we were in the dark, watching a movie. I didn't get to go to the movies very much. Most of them had kissing and killing in them and he said kissing and killing weren't for kids, even though he made a partial exception for fathers and daughters after story time. My daddy read stories like he was reading a script, every voice different. I liked *Hansel and Gretel* and the cunning trail of crumbs they left in the woods so they could find their way back to the woodcutter's house. Woods were my happiness. Coon lived in the bushes. The forest was so big he would be impossible to find. He had to find me again, apples or no apples.

My dad told me that the grandmother I never got to meet, because she'd already gone to the big sugar bowl in the sky, weighed over three hundred pounds. She lost one of her hands and both feet to diabetes and the doctor told her, "No more sweets!" That included her famous pies and cakes. Since she'd owned a bakery, going without was a real hardship. How could a person be around so much sweet stuff and not put it in her mouth? I couldn't. Most people couldn't. I know that. My gran kept right on eating in secret, but everyone knew. One day my dad staged an intervention and took her to a rest home. She hated that. The rest home inmates got bland food with no salt and no sugar and she was, understandably, driven mad by her cravings.

It turned out there was a male nurse at the rest home who was sweet on Gran. Either that or he felt sorry for her. That's what I thought until Stella told me in one of her drunken confidences that my gran was buying jellyroll. In extended care, deprived of chocolate, Gran was overtaken by febrile lust. (I could picture this behaviour. After Daddy died, the widow rubbed herself up against everything that stood in her way. I caught her with her hand in her panties lots of times, especially as she got older and less careful with herself.) It could be that my grandmother had mistaken kindness for perverse desire. Who in their right mind would want to make love with an old lady with both feet and one hand cut off? I had no idea. How was I to know when and why old people had sexual longings?

Gran hid her candy stash from the nurses and from my father, who said he had a nose like a bloodhound just in case I took it into my head to hide anything from him.

That was about the time my dad got Frend. One Sunday he took Stella and his puppy to visit my grandmother. It was a nice day. They ate their tasteless rest home lunch in the pee and Dettol-smelling dining room (now I know they all smell like pee and Dettol), and then took a walk in the garden. Just like the Queen, Gran took her purse everywhere with her, and she always wore gloves. They pushed her wheelchair past the roses and day lilies until Gran suggested a little nap under a big oak tree. Daddy and my soon-to-be female parent found her a place in the shade, put her handkerchief over her face, and told Frend to stay with her while they went off in the bushes for a little private time.

It wasn't long before my grandmother started hollering and Daddy and Stella ran back with their clothes all covered with prickles and leaves to find Gran cursing at the dog, who was running with her gloved fingers, still attached to her purse, in his mouth. My father ran after him and got the hand back, but it was all chewed up.

Later on, Frend threw up the chocolate. My father said dogs were allergic. Frend could sniff candy bars from a mile off. He ran at me from blocks away, and went straight for my pocket. My mother told me I got made in the bushes on Chocolate Sunday. They called me the chocolate miracle, because, since they got together relatively late in life, they didn't expect to be blessed with a child.

My dad used to say my mother smelled like baking and she captured his heart with her apple pie, the smell of apples and cinnamon. He made a big thing out of sniffing her neck and her hands. "Something's cooking," he said.

"You've been sneaking chocolate," he said, sniffing around my mouth, when I denied that I'd spoiled my appetite by eating before dinner.

Just as the scent of apples brought him the first time I saw him, I decided to capture Coon with my smells. I figured I was performing a public service. If Coon was stealing from us then he was stealing from everybody. If I trapped him, it would be a good thing.

Mr. Jung at the corner store didn't agree with me. I tried to get him to donate some fresh chocolate bars because kids stole from him too and I'd be doing him a service, but he told me I was a fat girl who made up lies. After that, I swore I would never go back to his place of business, but of course I had no choice. My mother sent me there to get her cigarettes and tonic water and she never gave me money. Everything got charged up on her account.

I taped a sign on the fence that said FREE CHOCO-LATE, ate a few stale bars and climbed the tree, careful to smear a little chocolate around my mouth. It never occurred to me that he couldn't read and magical thinking would be my real attraction. I believed that if I could keep a thought in my mind it was like a radio signal my father would pick up in heaven. He would do his best to make it happen.

I was trying to concentrate, but my brain was so full of jittery thoughts, I almost wiggled myself out of that tree, head first. The other big problem was falling asleep. I had a hard time sitting in the hook in the trunk without dozing off. I knew if that happened I would probably fall of my perch and knock my teeth out, or break a leg and there would be no help coming. By evening, my mother was usually so drunk she wouldn't have heard an elephant drop out of her apple tree. I would have waited there all night long, hollering like the tomcats that howl in the alleys of Kadıköy, and no one would have known. Even if they did, why would anyone in their right mind risk getting shot when they came in our yard to rescue me?

I talked to myself and went over songs I knew — trying to remember all the words and not just one or two lines – while night took care of its dark business all around me.

Why did my daddy have to die and leave us miserable females behind to do all this risky business? When would the grieving stop? I even went so far as hoping another man would come along and take my mother out for a spin in his convertible before it was too late and she made herself completely repulsive.

Sometimes my nipples hurt. Something was happening to my body and soon I'd be caught up in the same terrible need that afflicted my mother. I'd take off like a cat in heat and leave her behind. Who would take care of her then?

When I was numb from sitting in one position for so long and just about ready to yell uncle to my curious demons, I heard the boards give way as something hoisted itself over the fence. I hardly dared to breathe.

Moonlight delivered Coon to me. I saw him clearly, sniffing the air. Who knows if it was my magic or just a compulsion to visit the scene of an earlier crime that brought him? It didn't matter. He was there. He was much smaller than I was, with a ropey muscular body and long matted hair that was full of leaves and burrs, just like Frend when he dragged himself through the bushes and long grass that infected his ears and made them stink. The boy creature was wearing a torn shirt and jeans and a pair of new running shoes. Coon later told me that clotheslines were his haberdasher's. He showed me how he pinched his shoes from back porches.

As soon as he got near the base of the tree, I was going to jump and land hard, so his arms and legs would collapse under him. I was a big girl, and, tough as he appeared to be, I would have the advantage of surprise.

That wasn't necessary. As soon as he saw me, he froze. That was it. I had him. "Hi," I shouted down to him. "I am a mad mother; and from now on I'm the boss of you."

HEESE

I grew up hearing different music. When everyone around us was listening to the British Invasion, my parents were stuck in the radio groove of their coming of age. I think being the child of older parents made me different, apart. My mother and father had a whole bunch of favourite songs. One was "Paper Doll" by the Mills Brothers and another was "Some Enchanted Evening," from the musical *South Pacific.* I saw the movie on TV. At first I thought it was about singing fish – salmon chanted evening. On Sunday evenings, a dark night at the movie theatre, they put on their long-playing records and danced in the living room cheek to cheek. I would sneak out of bed to watch them. The dancing gave me split feelings. One was comfortable and the other wanted to get between them and break it up. I liked riding on Daddy's feet. He was *my* dancing partner, not hers.

When he told me that the tickling game we played at bedtime was the best part of his day, I thought that meant he loved me the most. Our songs were better than their songs. Ours moved quickly and some of them were funny old tunes like

"How Much Is That Doggy in the Window" and "She Wore Red Feathers and a Hula Hula Skirt." All the songs Daddy and Stella liked were about falling in love and never letting go. I thought that was sick. We are supposed to let go of dead people. What good are they? They can't wash the car or take out the garbage. They can't fix a broken girl.

A broken shoe ruined my mother's goodbye. When the hospital phoned to say Daddy had suffered another heart attack, she dressed up as if she were going dancing: crinoline, high heels, perfume – date perfect, while her taxi waited. But it turned into a pumpkin. In her rush, she tripped and snapped a heel. By the time she'd run back in the house and found another pair of shoes, Daddy had slipped right by her in the arms of another woman.

I know he loved us best, but my father had been slightly deranged by war and the availability of comfort women happy to trade their bodies for silk stockings and the Canadian rations soldiers packed in their kits, alongside the government pamphlet warning about venereal diseases.

When he died, our life fell apart. My mother needed to move on from grief and I was trying to take care of her. I had the idea of getting her a new dance partner. Then she might start acting like a mother again and I could have my old name back. Her calling me Mother and expecting me to take over her job was really wearing on my nerves. She was supposed to vacuum the carpet and feed me and Frend, my canine therapist, according to the Canada Food Rules, which I knew darn well included three vegetables, three kinds of fruit, whole wheat bread, milk and meat every day. Mystery meat and Wonder Bread sandwiches was no way to raise a kid and her dog. I wanted my mother to put her apron back on and start making chicken divan and chocolate cupcakes with Smarties on top!

My complaints campaign against candy companies that short changed kids with smaller bars had been so successful, I knew I had what it took to organize any kind of business from corporate rip-ons, my free stuff, to child finding. If I wanted to get the goods on my new midnight friend, all I had to do was put up signs all over town and knock on doors. He had to belong to somebody. The thing is, he hadn't told me one thing about himself that I could call a clue. As far as I knew, no one saw him but me. Maybe I was going through the same thing as Stella, who talked to my father and sometimes danced by herself while kissing the air around her. Maybe I was crazy lonely too and Coon was just a slice of moonlight that I could fold up and put away in my dress-up box.

If that was true, I didn't want anybody else checking out my untidy brain. I didn't bring kids home to play and I didn't let on how bad things had got at home. As far as anyone at school knew, I liked having the same lunch every day and it was only lunch after all. I had real meat, three vegetables, three fruits and milk with my dinner, didn't I? Who could tell that my white blouse got washed in the bathtub and pressed flat in a towel under my mattress the night before picture-taking day? If people found out that my surviving parent was drunk all the time and I was a one hundred percent orphan, the child welfare people might take me away. That was the last thing I wanted. Stella was all I had, except for Frend, who was way past his expiry date.

The summer before Coon, I worked out my plan to get my mother back from her orbit with a corpse. Calling her down was no use. The only thing that was going to work was to get her a boyfriend who would marry her once he found out what a jewel she could be. My daddy used to say that. "Your mother is rarer than rubies," he told me, while she made fried egg sandwiches for his breakfast, and the blood from his careless shaving got soaked up in little patches of toilet paper he stuck to his face.

I knew all jewels needed polishing. What Stella required was the right touch, the romantic equivalent of a rock tumbler, to bring her back to her former glory.

I made about a hundred handbills that said MAN WANTED in big red letters across the top and had a picture I drew with a write up underneath that said, "Stella needs a husband for herself and a father for her lovely daughter Madeleine, who is no trouble because she reads all the time. A fresh-baked widow who owns a nice house and car, she has insurance money and she likes to dance. Call 303-7251 and ask for Mother."

The hard part was the drawings. The pictures of my mother took forever. I had to be careful to make her face big and pretty, but not so gorgeous the guy would be disappointed when he saw her in the flesh. On the other hand, I didn't want anyone to pass by the posters thinking I was trying to get rid of dehydrated kittens.

I stole some money from Stella's purse, paid a couple of kids I knew to take the bus all over town and put up the ads, and postered our neighbourhood myself. Who knows whether or not my employees did their job? When nobody called, I started to wonder if they'd taken all the money straight down to Jung's. I went out and found Joey Leggett at the dirty bum slide, sat on him for a few minutes and rubbed dirt in his face. He didn't confess, so I had to let him go.

About ten days after the first poster went up, this skinny bald guy called Bill came to the door. It was in the morning and, miracle of miracles, my sleeping beauty was actually asleep in her bed for a change. I was glad the guy couldn't peek around the door into the living room and see her sawing off boards in the Easyboy. He said he was a photographer and he wanted to take my picture for the newspaper because I was a story. I told him he could snap away if he took my mother on a date. Bald Bill wasn't half as handsome as my daddy, but maybe he was a good dancer. I could hope. The guy said he would. He promised. "After," he said, so I went out in the backyard with him while he fooled around with his camera and a big umbrella.

"Take off your shirt," he said, and I said no. Even though I wasn't developed, it didn't feel right. Besides, I didn't like people to see me without my clothes on. I still don't. My body is my business.

"I'll take her to the Cherry Bank for dinner if you take your shirt off. This is an artistic shot. It's going on the front page of the weekend section of the paper.

"No way," I said.

"I have a great idea for the shot. I'm going to smear your chest with honey and, before you know it, you'll be covered with flies. No one will be able to tell."

I was half repelled, half interested in this idea. It was dumb enough to be compelling.

"Will they bite me?"

"Nah, we don't have the biting kind. They'll be licking the honey off you. Flies have tiny tongues. All you'll feel is a little tickle."

"I sure hope so."

"I've already got the headline," he wheedled, fishing a jar of honey and two Oh Henry bars out of his bag.

"Who are the Oh Henry bars for?" I asked.

"One for me and one for the first little girl to take her shirt off."

"OK," I said. I was used to bartering. My father gave me candy too. "Two candy bars and two dates, right?"

"Right."

The sun was high in the sky and I was covered with honey from my waist to my neck. I kept wishing for a glass of lemonade, but I had to sit still on the old kitchen chair Bill removed from the back porch. I was wondering if he was husband material after all. *Maybe not*. He was too weird. Bill put the chair between the big hydrangea and the fence, and it didn't occur to me that he did that so Stella wouldn't see if she happened to look out the window.

"How long do we have to wait?"

"Until the flies come."

They were coming, but not in any great numbers, just enough to irritate the hell out of me while they buzzed around my face. The poor things got their feet stuck in the honey as soon as they landed; so the numbers were adding up but not fast enough for my taste. Bald Bill was looking around the yard. He said he had to go for a minute.

Next thing I knew he was poking up under the eaves with the rake and a whole lot of angry wasps came out of their paper hotel to have a look around. I don't know what got into my head. I just sat there waiting when I should've run for it. In no time at all, those wasps came right at me. Bill had his camera in his hand and he was clicking away.

"Son of a bitch," I said, just like my father taught me.

"You're gonna be a star, Mother," he said. "Front page."

I ran in the house and banged the screen door as hard as I could. It was lucky I only got bit three times; lucky I am not allergic to wasps like some people and lucky I knew about putting raw onions on stings. My gin soaked housemate had a jar of martini onions in the fridge.

"An eye for an eye," my father's Bible said; and I too am a great believer in tit for tat revenge. I hid in the shade of the back stairs on the hottest Saturday in human history and thought up all the ways I could saddle up Bill and ride him into hell's fire without getting burned myself. First, I decided on dog shit. I would find out where he lived and cover his door handle with Frend's finest. I could take a lump of doodoo and put it in a paper bag and light the bag on fire right under Bill's kitchen window." Enjoy your dinner, Bill," I would shout while I ran down the street.

I waited for the phone to ring. Stella kept on keeping company with her virtual gentleman friends: Ed Sullivan, Edgar Bergen, Sid Caesar, Fred Astaire and Jackie Gleason, and I kept my head down. After a few days, it occurred to me that Bill was a fake. I picked up a newspaper when my mother sent me to the store for provisions. There was no Bill anywhere, no pictures, and no stories. He was just a garden-variety pervert.

I just folded up, and Stella got after me about my posture. "You're going to end up looking like a question mark, Little Mother," she said, until I wanted to scream. Who needed eye contact with other humans? I liked the ground better than the two-legged creatures that walked on it, the Bills of this world. I saw bugs. I found money. I skipped pavement cracks. God knows, we didn't need any more bad luck. I couldn't imagine how we would manage with a broken back.

My father once told me about a friend of his who'd broken his back in a motorcycle accident. The friend's mother had begged him not to get a motorcycle. He was an only child. She'd lost his twin at birth. It had choked on its cord and come out blue. After his accident, she'd come to visit him in the hospital, bringing a gift. When he opened the box, there was a toy motorcycle inside and it had been smashed to bits with a hammer. The next year at Christmas, he mailed his mother a doll he'd painted blue.

"What good did that do?" my daddy asked me and I couldn't think. Two people got hurt and nobody learned anything from it except it is easy to wound someone if you really want to do it. I got his point.

OSTLY LIGHT

E-mail to the motherboard

Ever since early man discovered the first reflective surfaces, we've been gazing at ourselves in mirrors. Vanity may be older than prostitution. Edison made it easier when he discovered how to paint with light. I have observed that many people keep their good photos and throw out the ones that are unflattering. I find the whole phenomenon of personal mythologizing fascinating. Everyone's snapping with phones now. Bad luck for the artists who used to make their livings painting portraits. Now Herat, home to the finest miniature painting, is an Afghani war zone.

I am the man Mad photographed with the bird. She will be surprised when she sees it.

There were no family pictures taken of Mad after her father died. If we are to believe her, no one apart from the pervert who attempted to photograph her half-naked bothered. Since I am mostly light, the way living humans are mostly water, I shall try to stay out of the way when Güzel points the lens at our friend. I don't think she would recognize me, but Mad is an intuitive person. It is my job to help, but not be seen, except as others. Visibility has complications, which she is discovering. She will say that she can't quite put her finger on it, but Güzel is not quite present, except in conversation. Sooner or later, she will attempt to touch him. I have been careful, but she senses my presence. I see her wrinkling her nose and sniffing. Our scent is ozone, but she thinks she smells orange blossoms, which the Turks make into the most delightful jam. Her little friend's breath smelled like apples. Many people have one acute sense that triggers the imagination. That is the beauty of being human.

I wonder if she knows that Iman's fiancé has married her in absentia, to restore her honour. She might object on feminist grounds, but what does Mad know about the reality of being a woman, even an educated woman, in this part of the world?

FIVE HUNDRED METRES

"Dress modestly." Güzel has phoned from the Hotel Metropol, which is directly across the street from the American Embassy, abandoned after the jihadist bombing, and invited me to visit the Blue Mosque with him this morning.

I have no idea what he means. Surely he doesn't intend for me to button up like the Kurdish women I see in the streets wearing headscarves, blouses, long skirts and overcoats that cover them from neck to ankles. I shiver at the sight of those dismal coats hanging like burial cloths in the markets. Whenever I pass shrouded women, I see the shapes of Pamuk's suicide girls hanging from headscarves in their grey dormitories, or the captive girls in the Topkapı Harem. I see Iman giving up the ghost in a closet in Tripoli.

I *have* been dressing modestly. In this heat I would go naked, given my druthers, but I have used discretion. At home, on those rare occasions when it is excruciatingly hot, I strip to my birthday suit. It is a nice suit, fits me well. I haven't bent it out of shape making children or eating myself to death. Not recently anyway.

"Don't show your arms or your breasts," he says, and I feel a current moving from my knees to my groin. "Breasts." What an intimate word. Odd that he should say it. "Breasts" was the first word I looked up in the dictionary when I learned to read. The dictionary didn't say breasts were prurient. I remember reading something like "the chest from neck to waistline." In those days, after the parson's nose, the breast was my favourite part of the chicken. Not any more. Now I like dark meat.

I will shower and then decide, I say to myself, but I already know what I will wear, to hell with the long coats.

He sighs again when we meet in front of the fish tank full of glum bottom-feeders in the Metropol, which is also down the street from the Pera Palace. I want to see the grand old hotel where so many famous people stayed, even though the fifty-lira price tag for high tea is outrageous. "What ugly fish. They look like undertakers," I say to distract him from judging my bare arms toned from giving hand releases to elderly gentlemen. I am wearing my black sundress with cross straps and a big straw hat. When I glimpse myself in the hotel window, I think I look more as if I am going to a garden party than to a mosque.

"You will be asked to cover your hair and put on a coat when we get there," he warns, me as we descend the hill toward the Galata Bridge after we've gawked at the stained-glass dome in the Pera and promised to come back another time for their expensive tea.

I want Güzel to take me by the hand and lead me over the cobblestones, which are hard to navigate in my platform sandals, but he doesn't. He walks quickly and I struggle to keep up.

"This is the old Italian quarter. Byzantium was the biggest market in the world. Everyone planted flags here. The tower was part of the Genoese fortifications. Now the district is so *touristic.*" He says the word with tolerant exasperation. My dress code has clearly ramped up his irritability.

A Muslim family passes us and I force eye contact with the wife. She does not return my smile. I am used to people smiling back at me. It is one of the prerequisites of an attractive woman. I enjoy it because, when I was an overweight adolescent, people looked at me with contempt or averted their eyes, as if I were an untouchable and contact meant contamination.

"Speaking of fortifications," I say, "the Muslim women do not look happy."

"It is hot," he says. I am sure I would get a similar reaction in the middle of winter.

"Would you believe I came here to hear the sound of the snow?"

"Because you were reading Pamuk." He rolls his eyes.

"Why does that bother you?"

"I told you. Pamuk has the perspective of Istanbul's upper class. That is not the real Turkey. Since he has had so much attention, he now says what America wants him to say, because America fawns on him, as they did dissenting Soviet writers during the Cold War. Now he lives in the United States half the time. As far as *real* Turks are concerned, Pamuk is an American."

"Do we stop being who we are when we are transplanted?" I ask. Isn't this why I am here? Do migrant birds have nationalities?

"It is more complicated than that. He is mistaken."

"What about the headscarf girls? Was he wrong about them?"

"He wasn't right or wrong. It isn't that easy."

"Is that a journalist's objectivity, or are you contradicting yourself?"

"Turkey is a contradiction."

"Is that why everyone is so polite, or are you afraid of insulting Turkishness?"

"Ah, Madeleine, you are beginning to understand. We are living on the razor's edge, some of us hoping for the simplest solutions, Occam's razor, but there are no easy answers in a country where half the population wants to be European and the other half Persian."

"Do you mean Iranian?"

"Maybe."

"What about Ataturk?"

"Exactly. Turkey is not ideologies. Turkey is food that tastes like the earth it was grown in. That is what Ataturk knew. A real Turk can close his eyes and tell you exactly where the bees that produce his honey have foraged. We are God's gardeners. That is the real religion and politic of my country."

"The formula for dirt."

"Exactly. The French call it *terroir*."

In the *Tünel* car, the oldest underground in Europe, we squeeze together. I am standing beside Güzel, holding on to a strap. When the train starts its rocking descent, I almost bang into him, something I would enjoy; but somehow he avoids contact. The men around us take notice. They almost smirk.

"Why were the men looking at me that way?" I ask, as we walk across the bridge.

"What way?"

"I don't know. Curious. Maybe judgmental."

"Don't people look at one another in your country?"

"Yes, but this feels different."

"You are nearly naked," he says.

"It is hot."

Güzel smiles when I quote him.

"Does your wife wear a long coat?" I ask, testing, maybe teasing. Perhaps he will reveal this important biographical detail and I will find out if he is worth pursuing as a love interest

"No," he replies.

"How far is it to the Blue Mosque?"

"Five hundred metres."

At the mosque, we take off our shoes, and, as promised, a functionary asks me to put on one of the dismal coats and replace my hat with a headscarf. Güzel offers to take a photo with my camera, even though I have told him that I do not like having my picture taken. The verger, or whatever they call such people in mosques, asks me to put it away, so I hold my little Canon in front of me and take a quick snap before returning it to my purse.

Later, I see it is a nice photo. This surprises me. I don't think narcissism is one of my vices, but I am pleased. But I am not alone in the picture. There is someone standing beside me. It is hard to tell if that person is a man or a woman. It almost looks as if he or she had his hands on my shoulders. Maybe I am imagining it. The hands could be light leaking from the stained glass windows.

I show Güzel the image in my digital camera when the verger turns his back on me. "I wonder who that is?"

"I don't see anyone."

"Do you operate on intuition?" We're standing under the beautiful blue and gold firmament in the enormous prayer hall. "Or, speaking of Occam's razor and St. Anselm, who had the best explanation, do you have evidence for the existence of God?"

"When I am in a holy place, I believe, because of the wonder of its beauty. When I am not, I have to trust Anselm and the limit of my imagination, reasonable proof."

"Does that make you a pragmatist?"

"We are all pragmatists in Turkey. The ones who were not were selected out centuries ago."

"Even the Muslims?"

"Especially the Muslims. They are farmers and shopkeepers."

"The customer is always right."

"Yes."

"Even the ones with their arms showing."

"The tourists with bare arms would not be asked to their homes."

"Would you ask me to your home?"

"Of course." I think he is telling me *his* first lie.

"How far is your home from here?"

"Five hundred metres."

"Can I buy you lunch?"

"I have already eaten, but I would be happy to sit with you."

I order. It is his country and he is clearly proud of its cuisine, but he waits for me to ask the waiter to bring dolmas, fava bean salad, yogurt, hummus, mussels stuffed with rice and the round *simits*, which I at first mistook for bagels though they are bigger and flatter.

"Would you like *raki?*"

I say yes because I am on holiday and I am nervous with Güzel. Normally I wouldn't have alcohol at lunch. The drunken shade of my mother dances on the wall opposite the sidewalk café. She is always there. Besides, a drink will make me sleepy and we always have at least five hundred metres to walk.

"We are going to visit the New Mosque next. It was built by a woman, the mother of Sultan Mehmet III, and once housed a school, a hospital and public baths. The Spice Bazaar was built to finance the mosque's charities. You people have the wrong idea. Islam is founded on the idea of community."

I am not "you people," not American, not English, Güzel, I think but do not repeat, because I have already told him, and if he asked me who I was I wouldn't have an answer. That is what I am here to find out. Trust is an acquired taste.

"Have you written about Iman yet?" I dare to ask.

"There are two women in my story, but don't ask me because I never discuss my writing until it is finished. It's bad luck, " he answers, and I understand I should not push him. I don't want to undermine Iman's journey with aggressive curiosity.

After lunch, we explore the Sultanahmet Spice Market. The humid mix of sweat, perfume and spices makes me drowsy. I am almost tempted to accept one of the innumerable cups of restorative tea on offer. Do the people who come out of their stores and restaurants to invite me inside think that I might be a plenipotentiary for peace, a Canadian angel hovering over Arab Spring; or do they just want to sell me something? I don't want a rug to take home. I don't want a belly-dance costume with veils and jingling coins. I don't want sex in a changing room. I want to know if God is good, or not, if I can live with goodness as a definition of the highest power. I want to taste *panis angelicus* with my invisible sister.

I smell my food. Having graduated from the alcoholic widow's menu of chip steaks and Wonder Bread to real food,

I am intoxicated by the earth smells of root vegetables and the aroma of plant pollens. Perhaps it is also memories of my father that invite such a complicated emotional response to culinary odours.

The spice shop is small and crowded with tourists. It smells like the hippy kitchens in vegetarian restaurants at home. "*Merhaba.*" A small man with a tooth-challenged grin bows his head, almost resting his crown on my breasts while grinding his groin into my thigh.

I jump back, bumping into bins of aphrodisiac cumin, oregano, and mint. The earth-coloured scents cloud the crowded space. "You are ç*ok güzel.*"

My clearly deranged spice guide advances, pushing crystal grains of sea salt into my mouth. "Good for sex," he says, indicating my *kuku.*

Güzel has warned me not to call out cuckoo when I mimic birds on the street.

"*Yok,*" I say, my useful word, backing out the door. The spice merchant scoops a handful of costly saffron, grabbing my wrist with the other hand. The hand stained with crocus pollen pulls mine toward his crotch. "*Yok!*" I repeat more forcefully, and stumble on the stone step.

A super-sized Amer-tourist, so huge he has to be a retired marine, catches me as I fall. "Thank you," I say, as Mr. Green Beret nods then nudges back into the throng with the ubiquitous American uh-huh. His wife has a tattoo on her arm. A few minutes ago I noticed her playing tug-of-war with a vendor inside the Grand Bazaar. "Will you take five? *Beş* for this homely scarf?" I love the way she said "homely" and imagine it hanging over the bare light bulb in the trailer home where she and her overweight hero might eat Twinkies and watch Fox News.

Bargaining is like foreplay for the merchants of Sultanahmet, the guidebooks say. This really turns on the middle-aged ladies with gold earrings that don't move. Never mind, the merchants have families to feed.

Güzel materializes.

"Did you see that?" I ask, trying not to sound annoyed and disappointed that he has left my rescue to a total stranger, especially one that doesn't fit my heroic concept.

"Yes."

I hold up my saffron-coloured wrist. "You'd think he would have been intimidated by you. Who in their right mind would feel up a woman with a male companion?"

"Perhaps he didn't notice me."

The spice seller is still standing on his stoop, blowing me kisses. I wish I knew enough Turkish words to rat him out with his wife.

Home Sweet Home

Coon had a line out near the Gorge rapids and we sat together watching the sunrise over Mount Currie. I'd filled my jeans' pockets with pebbles on the way up, but he told me he didn't want to take part in my stone-skipping ritual. He said he couldn't waste time playing. Being a kid was a luxury; and he had to feed himself.

"You'll scare the fish."

"These stones are for the water spirit," I said, offering him half of the cold chip steak sandwich I'd wrapped in waxed paper. My games weren't "play." They were necessary. If a ritual didn't exist, I invented one. My days and nights were separated by going-to-sleep rituals and waking-up rituals – mostly about keeping my room in order. There were no dustballs underneath my bed and no wrinkles in my sheets. Wrinkles would mean unexpected bumps in my life and I already had enough of those.

I sat on the bath plug because, if I didn't, our house would be deep-sucked into a sinkhole in the middle of the earth. I measured the distance between marbles and the space between hangers in my closet. Spaces were very important. Too little meant I couldn't breathe and too much meant I could fall through cracks in the earth. My room was spic and span. I wasn't going to let the tide of garbage invade my holy of holies. My father's First Communion Bible lay open on my bedside table. Every night before I went to sleep, I memorized a verse and I can still remember lots of them. That is the part of my father I choose to keep, the comforting words. Coon may have put aside his childish things, like St. Paul said, but all things childish are not necessarily foolish.

He had this way of appearing and disappearing. We didn't plan our meetings. They just happened. Either I would find him in the forest or he would turn up wherever I happened to be - only when I was alone, of course. My new friend didn't make it to school or any place where other people might have seen him. He had no interest in meeting my mother either. Why would he? If she'd given up on mothering me, why would she take a wild boy to her food-stained bosom?

The night I used my magic to bring Coon back to our yard, he promised to tell me who he was and show me where he lived. I swore not to tell. I told him I was the boss of all the bushes and he wasn't any different from any other kid. He had a funky smell. I thought I was going to gag on the stench of B.O. and pee.

"Don't you ever have a bath?"

He said he went swimming sometimes, but I found out that he exaggerated. Coon didn't really know how to swim. Of course, neither did I. After he caught a few herring, I dared him to jump off Dead Man's Rock into the Gorge. We dog-paddled in the dangerous waters, and now I wonder at our recklessness.

"Swimming isn't childish," I argued. "Keeping clean is adult work."

We dried ourselves with cedar boughs and set off into the evening. I guess I still thought Coon was just a kid gone wild for the summer and the part about living in the woods was pure fiction. I thought he was taking me on a shortcut to his neighbourhood, to a domestic situation even more broken than my own.

"Are you going to show me where you really live" I asked, as he kept going deeper into the forest and I followed right behind. I wouldn't admit it, but I was getting scared. It was dark. I could hardly see the moon or the stars any more, just glimpses over the top of the trees. There had been cougar sightings near Victoria that summer. One wildcat came into a yard and took a baby right out of its carriage. I heard about that on the radio. I thought I heard owls hooting and the sound of a big cat or maybe a bear sharpening its claws on an arbutus trunk.

"You're just slumming. I'll bet you live in a nice house with a swimming pool," I said hopefully, "and a freezer full of Fudgesicles."

Coon didn't say a word. He just kept on pushing through the bushes, letting the brambles and branches snap back at me. My arms and legs were scratched and I felt warm blood trickling and drying on my skin. I was going to look like I'd been through a cabbage grater in the morning. If Stella were to wake up sober, she would ask questions.

As if.

"I trust you know where we're going," I said, trying to sound threatening rather than terrified.

Of course, he did. Coon took me around and around in circles. If I had any brains at all I would have kept track of the stars, even though I could hardly see any through the dense foliage. He was careful to keep me away from open spaces until we ended up on some sort of bluff, a big rock covered with dry lichen and moss. Then he lay down.

"Are we here?" I half-believed we were because I was tired and didn't want to go any further.

Yes, we were here, so long as here is wherever we happened to be at the moment. He had that figured out. Here was where he wanted to be, and it was nowhere near home or whatever he called the two-garage suburban mansion or woodland shack where he lived. Here was where I was about to be abandoned. Coon lay on his back for a few minutes, watching stars travel across the night sky. I lay down beside him and closed my eyes, smelling the pine needles and cedar boughs all around us, and the salt-drenched ocean breezes. When I opened them again, he was gone, silent as sweat leaving the body.

Stay where you are, I told myself. Do not panic. I heard the mad singing of dogs and carnivorous nocturnal birds and folded into myself, my arms around my knees, and my head inside them. If I made myself very small I might not be noticed. I might be picked up by an up draught of air and floated back to my bedroom window, which I had, fortunately, left open. So this is how people begin to die, I thought, wondering if my father had left his heart on the same high rock in the forest behind our house. Was I dreaming myself closer to him?

I called out. "Daddy?" Then again, "Daddy, you boneless trouser snake." I heard my mother say such things when she was drunk. "You bastard. How am I supposed to get through this night all by myself?" My father was the one who'd carried me back to bed after I got lost sleepwalking. He was the one who'd held my hair back when I threw up and gave me little sips of ginger ale afterward. Where the Sam Hill was he now?

I fell asleep crying and woke up shivering at the first light, my eyelids stuck together by grief. The sun loomed big and orange over the treetops, climbing into blue sky. I figured I was due north of my house because the sunrise was to the left of me. Maybe I could get home on my own. Maybe I couldn't. My mother might not notice I was gone until she got hungry and called out for a chip steak or a cup of instant coffee. Coon was an asshole. He'd broken his word and he could burn in hell. If I died in the forest, he'd be damned. My father had told me about the damned, his face contorted by memory. They are hot all the time and there is no water down there.

I was parched.

I kept on being thirsty for quite some time. I guess Coon felt sorry for me. He came and got me just when I was deciding to take a chance and follow the sun home. It turned out he was there all the time circling the bluff. I could see where he had trampled the grass when he helped me down. I don't know if he slept at all.

"Why in hell did you do that? My mother must be going crazy wondering where I am. And what about yours?" He had me by the wrist and he was pulling me through the brambles again. My legs were really shredded now. They looked worse than the time I got impetigo after breaking out in hives from eating too many strawberries in old man Pritchard's garden.

Halfway down the hill we stopped and picked some huckleberries. I imagined my mother making lemonade. When I closed my eyes, I saw dew forming on the glass pitcher. She would leave out the pitcher, a cold glass from the fridge and a plate of gingersnap cookies, just in case I was hungry after going out to see the sun rise from the top of the hill. That's what I would tell her. I wasn't going to tell a living soul about Coon. Coon was nobody's damn business.

After Coon left me about a hundred yards from our house, I slipped through a hole in the fence. My private gate was hidden in brambles, but that didn't matter. I was already scratched to bits. The day was new, with dew still on the lawn, and our neighbours' vehicles enjoying the last moments of shady sleep in their carports.

I crept into the kitchen through the sliding door on the deck, which I'd left open the night before. There was no lemonade and no cookies. I grabbed a few slices from the open package of Hollywood Bread and stuffed them in my mouth.

Stella was in the living room, asleep in the Easyboy. First, I turned off the TV, then I covered her with the mohair blanket Daddy had given her to keep warm at his soccer games. Stella looked pretty when she slept. It was as if a big eraser had wiped all the sadness off her face. She had pink skin like the inside of a seashell. There was this feeling like a fist, part mad, part sad, in my throat when I looked at her. I wanted her the way she was before, but I didn't know how I was going to pull that off, short of a miracle.

I got into bed and had myself a big think before I fell asleep that morning. I had found a friend, but he had boundaries. I would have my own. If his house was out of bounds, so was mine. If Coon wasn't going to let himself be trapped, then neither was I. I liked mystery stories. Before I moved on to adult books, I read all of the Nancy Drew and Judy Bolton mysteries. I even read the Hardy Boys, even though it was more fun reading about girls. Coon was my private mystery.

We kept meeting on the high rock near the rapids and other places. He came and went. To keep my bearings, I got myself a five-finger discount compass at the corner store.

It started when Mr. Jang refused to put candy bars on Stella's charge account.

"She doesn't cook," I yelled at him. "What am I supposed to eat?"

Mr. Jung picked up a handful of snow peas and shoved them in my face.

"Eat, *gong*," he shouted back.

"But it's all your fault." Mr. Jung was a junk food pusher. He got me going on free candy when I was a little kid and now he was acting all high and mighty.

"I know about people like you." The cops had been to our school with stories about evil men who gave you your first funny cigarette. Truth is, he also got me going on Classics comics, which kick-started my addiction to serious books.

I felt better about going deep into the bushes when I knew I could find my way home. Coon knew every stone and tree in the woods but he wasn't going to be at my beck and call. That was clear. He liked surprises.

That day, I slept until Stella asked me to make her a chip steak sandwich for dinner. I didn't know that would be my new pattern. For the rest of the summer I slept during the afternoons and stayed out all night. If Stella noticed, she didn't say anything to me. Not one word.

I ran into Coon at my secret blackberry patch at sunrise one August morning. I wasn't surprised to see him there. He knew where to find all the free food. My patch was special because it grew around rocks and it wasn't hard to access the tops of the canes. We'd had lots of sun and rain that summer and the blackberries at my patch were big and tender, not dusty like road berries. Coon's mouth was stained a dark purple. His old syrup can was full when I got there. I told him I was making pie, which was a lie. I just wanted him to think I had to take my berries home, so I wouldn't have to share them with him. I felt bad when he actually helped me fill my bucket.

"You want to go swimming again, Coon?"

We took our berries to the Gorge and hid them in some salal while we splashed in the shallow water at the beach near the rapids. I wanted to ride the current right through the narrows, but Coon wouldn't go with me. So what if we drowned? Who would miss us? Maybe Coon had plans for his life, but I didn't have anything pressing going on in mine.

I thought one of three things would happen. One, I would have the thrill of my life riding through the rapids. Two, I would get sucked under and meet up with my father. Three, I'd get a closer look at where he went and come back and tell Stella about it. How could I lose?

He started dog-paddling toward the Tillicum Bridge and I followed him. When his head was wet he looked like a sea mammal. Hard to tell if it was Coon or a seal that came bobbing up for air every minute or two. The water was warm and salty. It held me up. I turned on my back and watched a family of seagulls attacking an eagle. It looked as though that eagle had taken a baby seagull from its nest. What a lucky baby to have so many mothers rescuing it.

What would Stella do if somebody or something came and took me away? Would she phone up some of the neighbours and go fighting for me like that? In the end, the seagulls won and the eagle dropped whatever it had in its mouth and went back to its nest in a tall cedar tree.

This was the first time we'd been naked in daylight. When we lay on the hot rock drying ourselves, I tried not to look at Coon, but I saw a few things. For instance, he didn't have hair down there like I expected. Now I know that girls develop faster than boys, but I didn't then. I had a bit of moss on my privates and some under my arms too. He had a brown mark on his stomach.

"That's where a fairy kissed you."

We watched dark clouds gather overhead and ate all the berries we picked. First we ate mine and then we ate his. Coon pointed out a hummingbird that stopped still on a branch and opened its mouth to swallow the first drops of rain.

"Do you live in a house?" I asked him straight out. "Do you have a mother and father?"

He didn't say a word. We put our clothes back on and walked back to the bluff where he left me the night I was almost scared to death. I didn't ask where we were going. I just followed. Instead of climbing up to the top of the rock, he showed me an opening hidden by bushes in the side of the cliff. It was the way into a cave.

All my life I had imagined caves, each of them different. I lay on my bed and made up stories to go with the cracks in the walls that I discovered in my rambles. Some of them were filled with treasure, the kind of thing I would expect to find in shipwrecks – gold bullion and fabulous jewels set in gold so dazzling I would need sunglasses. Some of them were filled with families sitting around big stewpots cooking over a fire. Others were abandoned mountain hotels with beds covered in goatskins carved in the rock. I also spent a lot of imaginary time with a family of bears hibernating in a cave near an abandoned orchard.

I found them when I noticed claw marks on the old apple trees.

Coon's cave was different from all the others. It was a real home with furniture and cupboards with dishes. He had blankets and towels and a braided rag rug on the dirt floor, which he tidied with a broom made of cedar boughs. I couldn't see so well at first, so he struck a match and lit a big stub of a candle. In the middle of the room I saw a circle of stones filled with ashes. There was a pile of wood neatly stacked against the wall. I bet our neighbours would be interested in knowing where their missing firewood went. He had a whole mess of it, and lots of broken branches for kindling.

When I nearly drove myself nuts looking for lost things in our junk heap of a house, Stella told me things had a way of finding the place where they were comfortable. They surfaced when they wanted to. A lot of stuff circled the world just waiting for the right wish. I knew Coon didn't waste a lot of time hoping for life's necessities to find their way to him. He hurried up the process by helping himself to sheets and towels and shirts from clotheslines and bits of furniture from garages, not to mention food from wherever it grew or was left by accident. His shelves, which looked as if they were made of old fence planking, were loaded down with cans and jars.

I recognized some things from our yard: our watering can, the missing green-stained boards from our fence, my Disney bed sheets and a wicker chair, just for a start. I felt mirth rise from my groin and fill my nose like a full on sneeze.

"You stole all this shit?" I said, all amazement and admiration. My crimes were petty compared to his. I thought of telling

Coon how I got treats to peddle at school by complaining about products that didn't live up to their advertising, but then I realized he might not be able to read, let alone write a letter that could convince a customer service person at a big company that he was some dissatisfied adult. That would be mean.

"Can I stay?" Hell, it was already like home. Between what he took from us and people I knew, I was already familiar with half his stuff.

Onion

Güzel phoned to tell me that he must leave Istanbul in two days. He will be covering large political rallies in Cesme and Izmir. "Isn't that where myrrh came from?" I asked, remembering this detail from my father's Bible.

"You could find out for yourself," he said. "I'm going to book the 8 a.m. Pegasus flight. If you want to come, we can make plans over lunch."

The restaurant he suggested is in the Galatasaray fish market. I quickly showered and put on a long-sleeved shirt and jeans. Yesterday, in spite of my conviction that I can dress however I please within reason, I'd felt uncomfortable when I walked through the waterfront district. Those fishermen have eyes like filleting knives. At home, we say it is the women who guard the rules and customs, passing on their folk wisdom and prejudices. In this country, it is the men who guard propriety. Why not? It is to their advantage. I wonder if this is the hard expression on the faces of Iman's captors. Probably. No doubt they had cooked up their self-justifying alibi about her bad character before they started in with her.

"You look better without makeup," he says, as I slip into the chair he is holding for me at the sidewalk café. I am pleased even though I know I shouldn't be. This is the face he would see if we were to wake up in the same hotel room tomorrow morning.

"Is your invitation to Izmir serious?" I had been planning to take the bus to the Aegean and Mediterranean coasts so that I could make good the first part of my promise to follow Sweet Papa Lowdown and their entourage on the tour south along the coast and then east to Kars, where Pamuk set *Snow*.

He tells me the Turkish buses are wonderful and cheap. I will have no trouble travelling inland after his work is finished. This way I could interrogate him and make unscheduled stops. I realize I am fooling myself. My secret agenda is not Ephesus or Sardis, the remains of Roman occupation. I am anticipating shared beds with Güzel in air-conditioned hotel rooms and perhaps using my rusty vaginal wrench to sharpen his pencil. He would use his powerful words to help Iman, and me too, of course.

"Why don't I rent a car?" I ask, imagining the opportunities that might present themselves.

Güzel answers, but his reply is drowned out by the dozen or so cats howling in front of the fishmonger across the street. "They have come for their lunch," he says, as the proprietor emerges with a large enamel bowl, which he empties piece by piece. More cats come running from alleys and shadows as he throws them the fish scraps.

"He feeds the cats at the same time every day." I have seen this phenomenon in every neighbourhood I have visited in Istanbul.

"Do any of these animals have a home?" Cats and dogs appear to be public property. Güzel explains, there are no rats in Istanbul. Millions of feral cats take care of that. It is hard to tell if their constant howling is the riff of hunger, territorial tail wagging or foreplay. These are the sounds I will remember: doves cooing, or cuckooing – which I have been informed is the name for female genitals – caterwauling and the muezzins regular call to prayer.

"Charity is holy law," Güzel repeats. "All creatures included."

Apart from feline theatricals, I haven't seen much drama in the streets, even during the electioneering that is following the Arab Spring in neighbouring countries. There is a sense of burdens stoically born. Even the Kurds carrying water and heavy loads of food, water bottles and mountainous trays of *simit* uphill, shrug at the summit. *İnṣallah*; hopefully they carry nothing but hope in the dreams that visit their brief allowance of sleep.

Although my guidebook warns me against personal assault, the only offence has been an occasional grope; and, coming from a youth culture, I choose to be flattered. I laugh at the tourists who wear their backpacks on the front like grotesque kangaroo baby carriers. They seem to be saying, Beware, Turks are thieves. These *yabana* women look ridiculous.

When I watch the evening news on my laptop, the American networks report pre-election violence. In the streets here, I have heard voices raised over the racket of car speakers playing rap slogans, but I have seen nothing that touches the animosity of American political discourse.

Speaking of which, I wonder if any Turkish movie directors have noticed how much Ataturk looks like the American actor, Kevin Kline. It would be such a waste not to use him in a film. He's amazing at accents. I wonder if Güzel could fix that? Is it magical thinking or is Güzel a general fixer, the plenipotentiary from heaven I imagine him to be.

Last night, I sat in a café where I could watch the street party after the local team, Fenerbahçe, won the soccer semi-finals. While I drank *çay*, I overheard a Swede and a Turk discussing the relative aging process of women in their countries, in English to my surprise. "Swedish women are beautiful," the Swede asserted, "but it changes overnight. You go to bed with a plum and wake up with a prune."

"Turkish women get big asses," the Turk contributed. "Like the Greeks."

I was dying to jump in and draw attention to their receding hairlines and slack stomachs, especially the Swede, but, in the name of Canadian diplomacy, I added another lump of sugar to my tea and sucked it up.

Despite the inauspicious start to my evening, I walked up the hill the fish market where thousands of Fenerbahçe fans were carousing shoulder to shoulder, singing team songs and waving flags while street musicians playing drums and pipes wove among them. Lacking the ant skills of 'Stanbul citizens,

I stalled in the gridlock of men. Not one jostled or called me *yabancı*. In fact, one inebriated gentleman took my arm and led me to a chair in an outdoor café, where I was given a glass of oregano tea. Another offered me a Fenerbahçe flag. No one drew attention to my ass or my wrinkles. When I checked my laptop, I found a *Huffington Post* news report that there were street riots where I was peacefully drinking tea. Go figure.

Random acts of kindness seem to be the social norm here. I have been offered countless cups of tea, helped with directions and witnessed animals fed by strangers. Beggars walk into shops and take alms collected in bowls. Sometimes the owners go straight to their cash registers and take out *bozdur-*

mak. These *bozdurmak* transactions are wordless. The first time I noticed this phenomenon I thought perhaps the shop owners were paying protection money, but Güzel reminded me of the Muslim rule, which is also a Jewish rule, mitzvahs are a cornerstone of community.

There is a blind boy who spends most days sitting by a storefront in Kadıköy. From time to time, people bring him glasses of *portakal suyu* from the juice stand on the corner or guide him to a public toilet. The whole neighbourhood is family. Yesterday, Güzel told me not to respond to street people. Later, he encouraged me to give all my change to a Roma girl carrying a baby in rags. I am confused.

"It is because you are a woman. You should give to women and children, not to men."

"I am having a hard time figuring you out," I say.

"I thought I was the interviewer."

"You are, but I need to know what you are thinking."

"So you would know how to answer." He spreads his hands on the table.

"Why would I do that?"

"Once again, because you are a woman, and you use female strategies."

"You are trying to annoy me."

"Yes."

"How un-Turkish."

"*Un-Turkish, anti-Turkish*. You are starting to sound like the government."

"Are you against the government?"

"I am *for* my people."

"Who are your people?" I say, before I realize that direct questions will get indirect answers.

"One of my people, a journalist, was arrested recently for insulting Turkishness."

"What does that mean?"

"I wish I knew."

"But you didn't mind when Pamuk was prosecuted for the same thing?"

"I always mind when freedom of expression is threatened. The president said, 'It is crime to use a bomb, but it is also crime to use materials from which a bomb is made.' I assume he meant words." He indicates a cyclist pedalling by the café. "I believe words are the bicycles of peace."

"So many contradictions."

"Welcome to my country." He laughs. "And you should know Turks dislike broken money."

"What does that mean?"

"It is beneath us."

We have been grazing the *mezzes*, yogurt, beans and *lak-erda*, finely sliced smoked tuna. The waiter removes them as soon as he thinks we are not paying attention to our plates. I say that someone could make a fortune selling food and drink clamps to tourists. Last night, a hotel waiter confiscated a full *raki* when I turned my back on it. And it had cost me ten lire. No more, because no one tips here.

"In Canada, most of the waitpersons are women, except in high-end restaurants." Our waiter smiles, appearing to understand what I am saying even though he doesn't respond to my request for water in English. I ask again for *minerale su* and still he doesn't bring it.

"Would you please ask him to bring some mineral water?" I ask Güzel, as the *levrek*, a charbroiled sea bass, is served. "What is this?" I separate the cucumber and tomato salad from my fish because I don't like food touching, isolating a mound of sliced onion with dark specks sprinkled on top.

"Onion with *sumak.* It is delicious."

He is right. The onion cuts through the fish oil and my obsessive compulsive agenda. We agree to walk through the Kadıköy fish market after lunch in search of *sumak,* which is related to a poisonous plant that grows in Canada.

"How is Turkey like an onion?" he asks.

"You are going to tell me."

"No, I am not going to tell you anything. You will learn by observation. We Turks are enigmatic for a reason. You never know who you are talking to."

"When will I get to the very inside of this onion?"

"That is just air. It is journey that matters."

The market smells about one hundred times as intense as natural food stores at home. I love the combination of spices, fish and fresh produce. When Güzel leans close to me, I can smell Europe and Asia mingling in the same kitchen. And orange groves. I breathe in and I think he notices.

"You see," he says, indicating nuts in labelled baskets. "Every nut has its own name. We don't say hazelnut, peanut, walnut, but we understand they are all related."

"What about the nuts in headscarves and long coats? Is there a word for that?"

I know it is presumptuous of me to pass judgment on a culture I don't understand. I sound like George Bush when he talked about freedom before bombing the bejesus out of Baghdad. What does he know about freedom? What right did he have to express indignation about weapons of mass destruction when his country dropped an atomic bomb on Japan? How many cultures will America destroy before their God gets their number and puts an end to their arrogant assumptions about good and evil? How can I even begin to know what it means to be a hidden woman, erased by my clothing? Is snow excreted by the devil to keep us quiet or, by god, to help us endure the darkness of winter?

What will I find in the market or anywhere else for that matter? Güzel tells me the nut vendors advertise Turkish delight as a male aphrodisiac. Will he be insulted if I offer him a piece?

⁓

My father taught me the difference between lookers and seekers. "Seekers," he said, are restless, always looking for the next thing. "Lookers" are the patient ones who wait for mysteries to reveal themselves. I thought it was confusing because he also called beautiful women, especially supernatural women shimmering on the silver screen, "lookers," but now I get it. The lookers wait like barnyard hens because they KNOW they will be found when the time is right.

This is what I am thinking while we stand in the Church of Holy Wisdom, built be the emperor Justinian and converted to a mosque by the invaders in 1453, while Europe took its eyes off the sacred dome of Christendom and focused its attention on discovering the New World. This huge room is the story of Byzantium with its layers of truth revealed and unrevealed, its deceptions and revelations all five hundred metres apart.

I want to weep. Güzel intuits my feelings and is quiet. I think this is what he requires me to feel in the temple of cosmic desire, where God is so close and still inscrutable.

I am waiting to be filled with the wisdom of the mother church, even though I have no idea what is hiding under the layers of Constantinople and Istanbul.

The dome of the Aya Sophia, which has survived earthquake and political turmoil, is covered in scaffolding. The Muslims plastered over the pendentives supporting the dome and now the government is having them uncovered. One excavation has uncovered an angel.

I want to ask Güzel what further glory they will find under the plaster, but I know he won't answer. I close my eyes and taste the fig pudding at Ciya, remembering that Musa told me food should hold onto the taste of the earth it grew in. Truth is the flavour in figs from the Garden of Eden, not far from here.

I hear the percussion of a thousand wings, as the temple doves all rise at once to circle the dome at prayer time. Then I see her, or him, the seraphim from the Book of Isaiah, a moon-faced angel with six wings.

I am astonished by the revealed seraphim in the Aya Sophia. Even before I looked up and witnessed the unveiled face in its labial nest of wings, I knew I would be surprised. It is an image of Iman. Does Güzel also see it? Should I wait for him to read its significance, or will he think I am out of my mind? "Hello," I say, echoing the Turkish schoolchildren who spoke their only words of English to the *yabancı* lady in the church of many incarnations,

"Hello. What is your name?"

She does not answer.

Her face, peeking out of a feathery surround, looked like a head about to be born. Is this the way angels enter cracks in the firmament, through a process like birth? Is it painful entering Earth's atmosphere? I have seen the same expression on the red and wrinkled faces of newborn babies. They seem to be saying, "Have I come to the right place?"

On the hill that leads from the Eminönü *feribot* station to the Church of Holy Wisdom, I saw a *simit* seller wearing a T-shirt that said in English, *How can I be lost if there is no place to go?* Where is *no place*, I wonder? Did the seraph also read it from her lofty vantage point? Did this statement of despair or resignation disturb her?

This angel means business. She has survived every indignity. There is no hope without moving forward, wherever that may be. If Iman, or Faith, has not yet found her freedom, I know now that she will. I am sure angels go back and forth for celestial rest and recuperation. The seraph, suffering the indignity of a Muslim cover-up, has worn a plaster veil for hundreds of years.

Did she just sit there listening, or did she go to a heavenly place to get over the man-created concept of exclusivity, so she could return for the Arab Spring of social revolution and the assassination of Osama bin Laden in his safe house filled with marching orders disguised as pornography and Coca-Cola cans?

Iman's mother said in an interview, "She is not only my daughter now. She is the daughter of the revolution."

"*Bozuk*," I say, and Güzel smiles. I think he sees what I see, an angel made from broken pieces of stone and glass, covered by men who believe the human face is a violation of holy intention.

" I knew you'd understand."

"Why?" I ask, forgetting everything I have learned about patience.

TUGRUL

Sweet Papa Lowdown is having a dinner and house concert at Tugrul's home before embarking on their tour. In addition to playing piano, sax, flute, clarinet, and risking extreme sports, Tugrul is a chef, a great one, Vefa says. Apparently, he has been offered a television show where he will ride his motorcycle to remote villages, cook the regional food and stay to play music.

I am intrigued when Vefa passes on an invitation to the party. Berk and Vefa will take us to Tugrul's house, which is on the European side of the Bosphorus.

"Can I bring my new friend?" I ask. "Is there room in the car?"

They are punctual. Berk is driving with Vefa beside him. "We could have offered one or two of the others a ride," he says when we get in the back of the Mercedes. I don't see a space.

"They're taking a *dolmuş*," Vefa says, and turns on the radio, which Berk aborts with an irritable snap.

"I need to concentrate."

He is right. There are no street signs and Berk says, since he has been studying in Sweden, he hasn't yet visited Tugrul in his new suburban aerie, if there can be such a thing in an ancient city. I am a bit disappointed because I've been hoping Tugrul would be living in an old family house, one of the wooden Ottoman mansions along the water.

Vefa laughs, and we cross the Ataturk Bridge in silence.

"I can't stand it," Berk says.

"Can't stand what?" Vefa asks.

"Who's chewing gum?"

"Not me," Vefa says.

"Not me," and I turn to Güzel, who says nothing.

"Berk has *misophonia*." Vefa laughs again and Berk joins him.

"It drives me crazy," he says.

"What?" I ask, as we drive over thousands of years of craziness: wars, occupations, misogyny and, currently, the sex trafficking of Russian children.

"He hates certain noises," Vefa says.

"So I became a musician." Now I am afraid. He is laughing so hard I think he is going to drive straight off the bridge.

"You won't be the first woman sacrificed in the Golden Horn," Vefa observes. Misogyny is becoming a theme with him.

This, I understand, is Turkish humour. Berk has an umbrella up his ass and so he prays for rain. Vefa, the philosopher, is distraught, so he plays the fool.

When Tugrul opens his front door, we are assaulted by beautiful smells. Rita, Cagdas's bride, on a break from interning in Berlin, is in the kitchen making a Portuguese *bacalhau* dish, and Tugrul's wife is nowhere to be seen. "She went to Rome on business." I wonder if she approves of this motley crew of blues men resting their *rakı* glasses on her grand piano.

"Cat's away," I say, eyeing the beautiful assortment of *mezzes* and bottles on the coffee table, and Tugrul winks.

"She'll be back," he says. "Who can resist handsome, talented and rich?"

"Me," says Vefa.

Dinner will go on all night, so they play first. Jeff sings "Doin' a Stretch" and then Sarp, the angel-voiced tartar, follows with "The KC Moan," so I think I'm in heaven; but then it gets better. When Rick starts to sing "Black-eyed Susie," the ubiquitous evil eye dangling from the neck on his mandolin, keeping time, Tugrul plays a sultry clarinet intro and then puts down his instrument. He doesn't ask. He just picks me up in his arms and floats me away. I close my eyes and pretend he's my dad. No wonder my mum couldn't let go. How many men make you feel like you're wearing wings, as if you are the lightest most acrobatic bird in the sky? We fly, and I don't want the music to stop.

But, after a few more songs, it does, and we sit down to dinner.

Güzel takes the chair beside me at the long table, which Tugrul tells us has been in his family for many generations and, when he was a bored six-year-old, he even carved his name in the wood during one interminable meal. No one speaks to my friend. Perhaps they disapprove of tourists picking up men in the market and the sort of man who will be picked up. Maybe they thought he should have owned up to chewing gum in Berk's car. The boys in the band and their assortment of wives, girlfriends and daughters are absorbed in their food and they talk about the tour.

Güzel doesn't seem to mind. I think he enjoyed watching me dance.

"How many people here believe in God?" Am I really saying this?

"I do," Hanna and Naomi, daughters of an apostate New Jersey Jew and granddaughters of a Baptist lay preacher, chime in unison.

"We are Turks," Vefa says after a pause, his answer, I am discovering, for everything, at once enigmatic and to the point.

"What do you mean," I ask, "this time?"

"I mean we are tolerant. We mind our own business."

"Since Ataturk," I say, and tactfully refrain from mentioning the Armenians.

"No, always," he replies, and turns to compliment Rita on her fish soup as Naomi tears a piece of flatbread and shares it with her sister.

The Ottomen, I am learning, are invisible and enigmatic, especially when it comes to religion. I wonder if this helps or hurts them when the earth moves. They have survived, so far.

The evening goes on and Güzel only speaks to me, explaining the conversation bouncing around us, and the food we are eating.

"That's pureed broccoli and pomegranate seeds with *dana bonfile. Dana* is beef. We eat cow, but not pig. The green bits are sautéed bay leaves."

"It looks like Christmas."

Several desserts follow this: baklava, pastries and puddings. Desserts are Tugrul's specialty.

"Try the *tavuk gogsu.*"

"What is it?"

"Caramelized creamy chicken breast. Delicious."

I am skeptical, but he is right, if anyone can be right or wrong in this country of contradictions. It is amazing custard.

"I love it, and I'll bet it ranks with chicken soup as invalid food."

"Turks never get sick." Vefa seems to enjoy my reaction to his little ironies. His friends are apparently immune. I must practice my non-reactive face.

There is lots of teasing and joking about the frustrations of life in a constantly re-invented nation, but no more talk of God or Erdoğan's gradual erosion of the rights and freedoms the secular Turks are no longer taking for granted. We leave after dinner, which has, as Berk promised, stretched to midnight.

When he walks me to the car, Tugrul kisses me on both cheeks and whispers, "What happened to your friend?"

I don't have time to answer. Berk has his earplugs in and he has started the engine.

"What did he mean by that?" I ask.

"We are all mad here," Vefa quotes the Cheshire Cat with a smile as wide as the Ataturk Bridge.

In the House of God

I asked Güzel if the dervishes live like monks – some of whom, tormented by sexual deprivation, are my clients. Do they find sexual fulfillment in dizziness? He laughed. Actually, I was hoping to flush him out. Since I have had my bottom pinched by a spice merchant and, more recently, on Moda Caddesi, by a dress salesman who looked like Omar Sharif, I wanted him to tell me why he hasn't at least brushed against me when the *feribots* lurch as they make their imperfect berthings.

I went by myself to see the dervish ceremony at the Hodja-pasa Hamam on my last night in Istanbul. I can understand why a Turk wouldn't want to witness such a *touristic* performance. Besides, Güzel says he's not a Muslim. Perhaps he is trying to maintain an ecumenical distance from the Sufis, who might be the Unitarians of the Middle East. In any case, I was glad to be alone. I didn't want this ecstatic experience explained to me.

The Mevlevi Sema Ceremony started late. I had time to examine the old stones in the *hamam* and the dome punctuated by stars. The front row of chairs sat empty until a tour of

Baptist-Americans came in and took their seats. I couldn't see past the wall of plus-sized ladies with enigmatic expressions, many wearing hats, from my back row position; so I stood up.

I wondered if Mohammad and Jesus were duking it out behind the impenetrable Baptist façades as they wondered if they were in the temple of God or the Axis of Evil. Despite the fact that we had been asked not to speak or clap during the ceremony, I laughed out loud during the reading from the Qur'an when I realized that the tourists, used to clapping during religious music, had been respectfully sitting on their hands.

I watched the dervishes, dressed in white shrouds with felt tombstone-shaped headdresses, circling their holy man, raising their right hands to Allah and pointing their left to the ground in a gesture of receiving and dispatching his blessing.

As the holy men turned to their sacred songs, I felt the message in their momentum. Let the music decide. If I had red shoes, I would spin to the answer. I'm remembering what Freya Stark, the poet of travel, wrote in her memoir *Ionia*, "Nothing short of the universal – the kingdom of heaven or the heart of man – can build the unfenced peace."

عه

It is very discreet, nothing obviously out of place, no papers flung about or missing, or cosmetics spilled; but someone has been in my room. I am precise with my things, especially when I am away from home. They are not exactly where I left them. It wasn't the maid. She was here with clean towels before I left the hotel.

I smell orange blossoms.

عه

When I check out of my hotel, praising the food prepared by Ahmet the owner, he frames his face with his hands and dances around the lobby. Ahmet, who has the countenance of a cherub, has exceeded himself with every meal. I decide not to tell him about my visitor.

"Someone was in my room last night," I tell Güzel, as I drive the Opel we rented in Izmir down the coast to Cesme. With its rolling hills and lush vegetation, the Aegean region could be Northern California with Roman and Greek ruins painted in the foreground.

He taps his shaved head with his fingertips, which I now know is his think gesture, but doesn't say, "Are you sure?" because I can see that he knows it is true.

"I'm sorry."

"Why are you sorry? You have an alibi. You were with me."

"I'm sorry because they may think I am passing papers to you."

"Who are *they* and what kind of papers are you talking about?"

"My novel."

"Should I start smoking so you could collect the butts?"

"I won't be creating a museum."

"Are you insulting Turkishness?"

"Of course."

A herd of goats appears from nowhere, and I manage to stop in time. I now imagine a car accident. Another group of anarchist animals will appear from nowhere. I will swerve to avoid them and we will be sent off a cliff into the Aegean Sea. Güzel's wife will read about it in the *louche* Technicolor newspapers. I wonder if he writes for them?

"Who do you write for?"

"Myself. I am the only reader with integrity."

"What will your wife think when she reads about our car crash?"

"I am not married."

"I thought you said you were."

"No, you asked me if my wife wore a long coat. I answered no; my wife does not wear a long coat because I do not have a wife, not in this life."

"Ah," I say, not quite understanding but unwilling to intrude further as we ride in silence, until Güzel tells me to stop for lunch at a roadside café, where I order lentil soup and foamy *ayran*, practicing my menu-Turkish.

"The less you know about me, the better," he says, as I finish my glass of tea. "Through me you will find out about Turkey and from you I hope to learn how the world sees us. We both need to be transparent in ways that are helpful."

"What's the point of that? I am a very unimportant person. No one cares what I think of food or politics or anything else. I am a tourist, here to find out what Pamuk meant about hearing God in the silence of snow and hoping someone will help a woman betrayed by her culture." I don't add that I am also here to get rid of my father's ashes. That is too many reasons, my father would have advised. One is enough. More, and you appear to be lying.

"You came to listen to our snow during summer?" he smiles.

"I came when I could." This is my first trip abroad. I have never been anywhere except for annual ferry trips to Seattle and one trip to Disneyland on a client's Harley. It is now almost three months since the rape and the world has turned its attention away from Iman.

"Where is Faith?" I ask.

"Don't you understand that is the same question we are all asking? How will any of us hear God in the clash of civilizations? You will have your journey, and I will write about it."

"What if I don't find any answers?"

"One thing we have learned in thousands of years of history is that it doesn't matter. We don't have goals the way you do in your culture. Time is irrelevant to us. Turkey will be here long after we have passed through life. What matters to us is the next cup of tea, the pomegranate flowers, and the scent of our pine forests in summer."

"Are you really writing about the elections?"

"*Bakalım*," he says.

"What does that mean?"

"We'll see."

I live on a fault line, as do the Turks. The earth will move in spite of us. There is no magic, no politic to prevent the tectonic dance that is our destiny. Is this what he is telling me, that talk of white and black Turks, Christian and Muslim Turks, Jewish Turks, deep states, the invisible power, and visible governance, is just talk? Is life about not stepping on cracks?

اللَّه

If possible, we saw even more election flags in Izmir than in Istanbul.

"Western Turkey defends secularism. You'll find the dedication gets more intense as you move down the coast. " Güzel wanted to press on to Cesme where there is a rally this evening. On the drive along the peninsula to the seaside city I smell the famous pine forests through the open windows.

"It smells like heaven," I say.

"This *is* heaven," he answers. "Ask any Turk and that person will tell you that he or she would die for his country, just so he can get to stay here." I notice he says "will" and not "would" as some people do when talking about their nation, their children or a special friend. Is that conditional? Many of the Turks I've been meeting talk about emigrating if the Prime Minister moves any further away from secularism. Many have already. "What will happen when politics, religion and climate change force the great Middle Eastern diaspora? How will your people live without pine forests and fresh figs?"

"We will live our way to the answer."

I park at the end of the highway to Cesme, and Güzel heads straight to a boisterous rally in the square beside the Castle of St. Peter, a stone fortification built by the seafaring Genoese in the fourteenth century. At the Dinc Hotel, close enough that I can hear the massed crowd, I ask for two rooms on the same floor, facing the Aegean. The proprietor looks surprised by this Western woman making her own arrangements and gives me one key. I wish I could give a false name because now the government knows about me, but it is impossible. I have to hand over my passport at the desk.

After dumping my bags, I decide to walk over to meet Güzel near the speaker's platform. The square is full of people. A howling child has dropped her ice cream and a small dog is licking it up. There are three trucks parked in the square with the photos of three different candidates painted on the sides. All three loudspeakers are blaring at once.

"How can anyone hear what they are saying?" I ask, covering my ears.

"They already know all the platforms."

"I'm going to walk along the seawall and watch the sunset." There are so many people taking pictures. Someone might be waiting to get one of us together, evidence of conspiracy or if, in fact, Güzel is married, evidence of adultery or intended adultery. I am getting paranoid.

I have never seen such glorious sunsets as in Turkey. It is not hard to believe the Turks have chosen a little slice of moon and a star for their national flag. I walk for five hundred metres, yes, I count my steps, until I no longer hear the election speeches. At a café by the water, I order an *ayran* and a fish sandwich, and then wait for the sun to drop out of sight.

Further along the beach, tourists lying on huge cushions in cabanas on stilts in the water also watch the sunset. I can hear their laughter. One couple is kissing, their shadows playing on sheer curtains. I let myself imagine.

At the end of my promenade, I hear the sound of a trombone and follow it into a restaurant with Turkish carpets and low tables with water pipes. The walls are open latticework covered in grape leaves and there is a refreshing breeze from the sea. What a magical theatre, I think, and, sitting near my blues band, I order an *Efes* beer. Jeff nods to me and begins to sing "Lost Lover Blues." Am I ever!

During the break, he asks why I didn't bring my new friend to his gig.

"He's making Turkey," I answer as simply as if it were Thanksgiving dinner. It is true if we believe what we read.

♪

I am in bed studying my *Eye Witness to Turkey* when Güzel taps on my door a few hours later. "Have you had dinner?" he asks and I say yes, I have. "Well then, I'll keep working. Would you like to swim in the morning?"

Of course I would. I blow him a kiss through the closed door. Do I hear him catch his breath on the other side, or am I imagining it?

Bakalım. We'll see.

FAIRY TALES

Coon told me all about his life and I told him about mine. I was surprised by what he knew and what he didn't. He was smart and completely clueless at the same time. When we heard dynamite blasting the rocks in a new subdivision not far from his hiding place and I said, "Duck and cover," he didn't have any idea what I was talking about. But, while Coon knew less than nothing about war, he knew every inch of his woodland kingdom, every bush and berry, every squirrel, I swear. His mind was a map, even of the houses on my street. He knew who had fruit trees, who left their basement door open, and who had shelves full of preserves ripe for the plucking. I have never met anyone wiser about plants and animals and five-finger discount shopping than Coon.

Most important, Coon was familiar with grief. He had experienced death early, just as I had. Since we'd sworn to be true to one another and never lie, I believed his story. There was no big fancy house, no mother, no father, no brother or sister, not even grandparents. I had half my grandparents, even if they did live far away in South Carolina, Freedomland. I could picture them.

He told me he'd started out someplace cold. He remembered seeing red splashes in the snow. His father broke his mother's nose before she ran away with him in her arms. He'd looked over her shoulder and seen a trail of blood following them. I asked him if he was sure about that. If she were carrying him, wouldn't he have been a baby? I knew from the kids I'd babysat that there comes a point when you can't carry them anymore and that is about the same time they start to remember things. That was when I had to be careful about how much I ate out of the fridge in front of them. I had this trick of eating their Jell-O with fruit in it. I would cut right across, a little skinny piece, and then the parents would be none the wiser.

"I was five," he said. "I remember everything."

Sometimes Coon's mother went back and sometimes his father found them, but one night, when he was drunk and raging, they ran away for good. His mum had experience waiting on tables. She took their old Pontiac and drove it right across Canada, trading work for food and gasoline and sometimes a bed. Most often they slept in the car or in motels. The motels were free when they got up before sunrise and booted it down the highway.

"My mother left every room nice and clean. We only used one towel, which she washed and left hanging to dry on the shower rod, and we slept on top of the blankets so they wouldn't have to change the sheets. That was her way of saying 'Thank you.'"

I believed Coon because I could see he might have inherited his mother's talent for housekeeping.

"Was she pretty?" I asked. It was important to me that mothers were pretty. My own used to be. She was older than some of the other mothers, but she was still the most beautiful. Crying and drinking had made her face puffy, but other than that she still had some female charms. Her drawl was partly from drinking and partly vestiges of a Southern accent. My father, who met her at a dance contest, liked to talk about her "great gams" and her "bodacious bootie." She was, he said, "a real tomato." I, of course, was not. I knew that. My face was not going to appear on the cover of *Silver Screen*.

I was too fat. "Just baby fat," Stella said. "It will melt off one day and then you'll be the belle of the ball." She was right, for once. I could have been.

My mother had lots of jewelry my father had given her. I was thinking of this when I came home from school one day and found her in a good mood. She'd actually made some Rice Krispie squares.

I asked her, "How many ways can you make a baby?"

"What do you mean by that?" she said, as she swirled her finger in the marshmallow and Rice Crispy mix and licked it off.

"I mean there's the one where his peeper goes in her peeper and the babies swim out. Right?"

"Right."

"This boy at school told me a boy can put his peeper in a girl's mouth and get her pregnant."

"Well, he lied to you. Either that or he was misinformed. You don't get pregnant when you do that. *That's* when you get jewelry." She laughed at herself and I wondered if those squares would be safe to eat. Since then, I have not been able to regard my mother's jewelry, except for the jet necklace, with any kind of respect.

Coon told me his mother was also a beauty. She had red hair and her nails and lipstick matched. I asked if she had jewelry and he said, no. His dad was poor. She had a wedding band and a watch. That was it. They lived in the Pontiac for a whole summer while she looked for work. Sometimes she brought guys back to the car, and he had to hide under her coat in the front seat while she entertained them in the back. "It's eating money, honey," he said she told him.

One hot day she said they weren't going to the beach like she'd promised. She had a job interview. He was supposed to wait in the car while she went in and talked to a man who was going to hire her. First, they went to a gas station where she had a sponge bath and washed her hair while Coon sat on the toilet and watched. He told Mad he'd spent a lot of time watching and waiting. Then, she parked across the street from a diner with a neon sign. It wasn't lit up. "Wish me luck," she told him as she kissed his nose. Then, she got out of the car and started to cross the street. Coon wasn't looking. He was watching a dog cross from the other side.

The guy in the black car must have been looking at the dog too, because, when he swerved to miss the animal, he hit Coon's mother.

Her blood spattered on the windshield.

The guy in the black car kept going. Coon got out of the Pontiac and looked at his mother. He said she had blood coming out of her like all those other times when his dad hit her, but more of it. The way he said it was flat, as if he was giving evidence, as if he'd gone over it a thousand times to himself. This time his mother was still. Her hand didn't move to take his and reassure him she was only playing possum so his dad wouldn't hit her again. She was dead.

"Wish me luck," she'd said, and that was when he found out he didn't have any to give.

He ran down the beach, across some streets, through some bushes, over the blue bridge; and he didn't stop running until he came to his cave.

Coon spent his entire life, from that moment on, living wild. His daddy hit his mother. A car hit his mother. The only thing that never slapped him in the face was nature. He trusted nature. I agreed with him one hundred percent. If a bee's going to sting you, it's because you got in its way. Just let a plant grow and an animal find its food and everything lives together in harmony. Why can't humans live like that?

I think of Coon's dead mother every time I cross the street in Turkey, but the only roadkill I have seen was a young woman in Kadıköy, a walking dead. The disfigured girl came and went with a traffic light near the *feribots*. I have no idea what hit her, but it could have been a bucket of acid. She was wearing a *hijab* but her face was uncovered. It looked like raw meat, but she held it up, defiant I thought, as her male companion led her across the busy street.

I couldn't believe a Turkish man would do that. She must have been a Pakistani, maybe in Istanbul for plastic surgery. Perhaps the man with her was the lover she had chosen against the wishes of her family. Maybe he was a brother, parading her so the world could see what men do to women who assert themselves. I would never know. Freedom has a very high price. Coon taught me that. Iman taught me that. The lessons are everywhere.

I was half jealous of Coon because he was living the freedom life. I didn't tell him, but if I didn't have Stella to take care of I would have taken off myself. Many times I lay on my bed thinking about where I would go if I had the gumption to get up and leave. I thought of the paper shack or an old garage like ours that was all overgrown with weeds. Robinson Crusoe was my hero.

I've heard that raccoons are related to bears. I guess they live in caves too. Coon didn't mind the name I gave him. Maybe, I thought then, he had a real one he'd forgotten because no one except me spoke directly to him after the day his mother was killed.

It might have been better if he'd been a bear person. His life would have been a lot easier if he could have hibernated in winter and foraged in the summer. In summer, there were fruit trees and vegetable gardens to raid and open doors to investigate.

He showed me where there was a baker who left his back door open in the heat. Coon just had to go under cover of darkness and sneak in the back way, taking whatever he liked. He stole bread, pies, cookies, cakes, pastries, and sausage rolls. The time I went in there with him, I had the hardest time deciding. In the end, I took a blackberry pie and it was delicious. We sat on the curb and ate it with our fingers. My blouse was black and blue from holding it against my chest, but I didn't care. I bleached the stain out later.

I made a promise that I would help Coon get through the next winter. I could take him stuff from our house and I could charge stuff at the store. Heck, I did it for myself. It was a comfy feeling knowing I could help somebody out. Stella mostly took it for granted when I cared for her. She was a bit of a princess that way. Coon was different. He didn't ask for help.

We talked for hours around the fire in his cave and toasted marshmallows, removing one caramelized layer after another. That was my idea. Coon didn't know about burnt sugar. "Think of it as underwear," I said. There were lots of things I taught him. I asked him if he missed his mum and he said he did. He asked if he could suck my nipples and I said no, because they were tender. I was too shy to show them to anybody, especially since I was getting ahead of the other girls in my class.

I'd heard some older girls in the school washroom talking about breasts. One of them told a story about a girl who wondered how she could get hers to grow. She said a mean girl told her to rub them with toilet paper every day. The girl went into the toilet cubicle and followed her instructions. A few weeks later, they were in the shower together after gym class. The girl who rubbed her chest with toilet paper was still as flat as a board.

"Didn't you do what I told you?" the mean girl asked her.

"I did, but nothing happened. Are you sure it works?"

"It worked on your ass, didn't it?" the girl said, and her friends cracked up.

What a dumb joke. Coon didn't get it. He wasn't used to jokes, and he didn't know any songs or poems or stories either. You could have blown me over with dog breath when he told me he didn't know how to read. School didn't interest me much. I already knew how to read when I got there. As far as I was concerned, school was a place where kids got to make fun of my clothes and my lunch and my husky shape. I wasn't exactly the teacher's pet type either. To be honest, I loathed getting up in the morning. By my definition, a good teacher was one that left me alone at the back of the class with my library books.

The next day, I brought a book to the cave and told Coon I was going to teach him to read.

Some kids are suckers for "happily ever after." We believe it because it's all we've got. Coon and I started with a fairy tale.

We sat down on a moss-covered rock near the door to his cave and tucked in.

"Once upon a time, there dwelt near a large wood a poor woodcutter, his two children and their stepmother," I began reading the story of Hansel and Gretel, because it fit us so well. As soon as I started reading, he put his thumb in his mouth. I had already noticed Coon's nails were bitten down and his thumb was shrivelled, like it had been in water all day long. He was still a little baby, one who was badly in need of a bath. Coon's hair was matted in dreads and he was filthy: in spite of plunges in the salt chuck and rudimentary washes in the rain barrel, he kept at a discreet distance from his cave. I didn't ask where he went to the bathroom, but I guessed it was everywhere. "Don't shit in your own well," my daddy used to say. That is why I was so surprised when I realized that was what he had been doing all along.

When I finished reading the story of hapless children abandoned to their fate in the forest, Coon asked me to read it again. So I did. When he insisted I read it a third time, I realized it was going to be hard work getting him to settle down to his lessons, so I decided the story would be his dessert. We would start with letters and sounds, and if he played ball then we could have story time.

I started thinking about fairy tales and how all the bad guys were stepmothers. Somewhere out there Coon had a bad dad. His mother was dead. At that time I believed I was the vice versa reversa. Would my prescription for Stella's loneliness backfire on me? Would the man of her dreams waltz into our life and step on my toes? That part had not occurred to me. I just thought I could find a dance man for her and a daddy man for me. If Coon's dad hadn't been a rat, all we would have had to do was find him and put him together with Stella. That would be a happy ending – me, Coon, Stella and what's his name. We could live in our house and, if he didn't have a car, we could peel the blackberries off the garage and get the old car going again. That would have been perfect.

One afternoon Stella interrupted my siesta, a nice daydream in which the four of us were posing for wedding pictures, Stella and me in matching dresses she'd made out of pale blue lace. She sent me to the store for lemons. It was too hot for gin. She had a hankering for iced tea. Since I thought there wouldn't be any change, I stole a pack of Popeye candy cigarettes. Mr. Jung came up to me where I was resting my head on a box of Popsicles and asked if I wanted to buy a bag of peas in the shell, my play cooking game, cold peas stirred in cold water from the garden hose, from before I charged candy bars and got husky and he took it on himself to become the fat police.

When I was a little kid, my mum would give me a nickel and send me to the store for peas. I filled a pot with cold water and emptied the pods in it.

I told Coon about my daydreams and he smiled so I could see all his stumpy teeth at once. "You should go to the dentist," I said, and he didn't have the foggiest notion what I was talking about.

"All the lost teeth go in the pearly wall around heaven, right?"

"That's baby teeth."

"So it keeps getting bigger."

"I guess that's the idea, people getting born, losing their teeth and dying."

"Making room on both sides."

BEATIFIED

E-mail to the motherboard

At Passover Seders, Jews ask the question, "How is this night dif-ferent from all others?" and then they tell one another the story of their flight from Egypt and discovery of the Promised Land.

Tonight I did something I have never done before.

It began on the seawall. I walked beside my client, smelling her hair, which she had washed in a jasmine-scented shampoo, and enjoying her pleasure at the full moon and the songs played by her Canadian friends and their Turkish bandmates at the café on the waterfront.

Mad was enchanted by the *cumbus*, our Turkish banjo-like fretless instrument whose metallic body makes the sound of light skipping on water. She stopped dancing to listen several times. I think she even ceased breathing.

I longed to speak with her, to tell her what I know about this particularly Turkish instrument that is a mix of Asia and Europe, just like this country, something the Father of Turkey recognized when he gave the *cumbus* its name, which means "joyful," but conversation is not my job. Güzel speaks. He is her teacher. I am his master. It is my job to listen and give gentle guidance, a hand.

Tonight, because she was ready, the moon and the music having worked their magic, was my time to make love to her. I followed her up the stairs to her room on the first floor and watched her hesitate outside the room she had reserved for Güzel, listening to see if he was awake. I slipped through the door after her and watched her step out of her dress and hang it up. While she was in the shower, humming one of the tunes she had heard during her promenade, I watched her slowly caress her body with soap and then rinse off the suds. Because the air conditioning affects her sinuses, she has left the system turned off.

Mad left her new cotton-lace nightgown hanging on the hook on her bathroom door and went to bed naked. Licking her fingers as she turned the pages, she read her Turkish *Eye Witness* until she heard him outside her door. Oh, she wanted him to come in. She wished she had put on her becoming nightgown and that she had the courage to ask him to join her. I watched her blow him a kiss.

In between the ordinary and the divine there are beatitudes that transcend taboos. All is mutable and every act is a prayer.

She took a long time to fall asleep. I waited, listening to the cuckoo coo of the doves on the roof and the sound of words on paper and thoughts of Güzel moving through her mind, until her eyes finally closed and the heavy book fell out of her hands onto the floor. I picked it up, marked the page with a hotel postcard, and turned out her light, then lay down beside her and touched her very gently, all over, the way she touches her old ladies and gentlemen.

She was having the dream where her father tickles her.

I have heard the delightful incoherent noises of Japanese girls when they are delighted by cherry blossoms or by the taste of green tea ice cream and American or English girls waiting at stage doors. Those are the chirping sounds Madeleine (I shall call my client Madeleine for the purposes of lovemaking because of the music, three syllables are music; and one is simply a note) makes when she is touched in her sleep. I would call those noises "joyful."

This is as new to me as it is to her. Angels don't normally make love to their clients, but I like the idea of awakening Madeleine to her own pleasure. She has only ever given. It is high time she received more than just a tickle, time she learned that pleasure can mutate from something as simple as laughter to the earth moving.

Madeleine's angel in the snow may be ecstatic release, but she is no ordinary sex tourist. I am going to call this lovemaking "touch." It is all in the hands. I swear I felt her spirit healing as I touched her flesh, every hair erect, every follicle shivering with pleasure. This is a private sacrament. My manual says that, just as she will wake up tomorrow morning unaware that her body has repaired and replaced cells during her sleep, she will not remember that she was loved, but she will look at herself in the mirror and see light passing through. I hope she will feel beatified.

BABA

While we enjoy our Turkish breakfast – tomatoes, olives, cucumber and eggs with *simit* – on the patio in front of the Otel Dinc, small finches clean up the crumbs around the tables. We have been given tiny bowls of butter drenched in honey. I swipe my bread through it.

"Did you know honey is bee vomit?" I ask, and Güzel shrugs.

He is very quiet. He filed his story last night, but says he couldn't sleep afterward, so he sat on his balcony and drank *raki* until the sun rose.

"Why did Ataturk legalize alcohol if he was a Muslim?" I ask.

"I ask the questions, Madeleine."

"You said I would learn about Turkey. That was not a personal question."

"Alcohol is a personal issue here. It is still uncomfortable, but we are practical. Tourists will want to drink on their holidays for one thing. I will tell you about a conversation I recently had with my father and an American journalist who visited our farm."

"Your farm?"

"My family grows olives."

He pushes the button on the recorder. I hear Güzel's voice first. "Baba, my American friend wants you to tell him what Turkey means to you. What are the three things you would tell this American about Turks?"

There is a moment's hesitation as his father clears his voice and considers his response.

"Everyone is our relation by heart. First, we expose ourselves, but not too much. Then, we offer hospitality. All Turks like to share what we eat, what we drink.

"And there are some more things." Güzel's father speaks as if he has pebbles in his mouth or congestion in his lungs. His breathing is louder than his voice.

"We are half Asians, half Arabs. We are half Balkanians, not a real Islam. We drink. We go to mosque. For some of us it is a great sin to drink, but in the Qur'an alcohol is forbidden, but no punishment. If you drink it is forbidden. It is a sin. That is all.

"During Ramadan, rural man meets with tourist having beer on the road, just resting. Man has been working hard and he is thirsty, but he cannot drink. He says to tourist, 'You may drink and I cannot, but we both take care of our religion.' That is the attitude in my country.

"In the Qur'an there is a great proverb. 'There is no one between you and God.' We are all responsible to God for what we do and do not do. The Arabs and the rest of the Islamic world hate us Turks. They say, 'You are not Islam.' They feel shame because of what we see on television. Everything is fear and they think of us as Christians.

"We are an oasis between Christianity and Islam. Turkey is place to rest and drink."

"That is beautiful, Güzel, but is it practical?" One drink leads to another, I think, and when the drunk is asleep, the house burns down.

"You should ask your parents questions like this. It is important."

"My parents are dead."

"Oh, yes, I know. I am sorry."

He is. I can tell. We've been wired to think community means continuity, and family is the first community. I try to think of something to comfort him, because I have embarrassed him by exposing my deficit. We are all supposed to have loved ones. Even Iman has a family that cares so much for her they will risk their lives to defend her honour.

"My father grew tomatoes and cucumbers. I am sure he would have had an olive tree if it could have been happy in our climate."

The foraging birds fill the silence between us, and I feel fire. I can't be having a hot flash, not yet. I pick up my napkin and fan myself.

"It is so warm, I can't tell whether or not I am having a hot flash."

"You are joking."

"Why would I?" I think he wants to ask me how old I am, but I know that he will not. "It isn't a power surge."

Later, when we are lying in the beach cabana with its long sheer curtains blowing about us after swimming five hundred metres out to sea and back, I tell him about meeting Coon the summer I was twelve.

"You know," I say, "he had a birthmark in exactly the same place as you, on his stomach."

"Long ago, a fairy kissed me."

"What is your father's name, Güzel?"

"Sevmek."

I close my eyes and listen for the sound of angels in my bottle tree. It sounds as if they are arguing. Is this the battle of the apocalypse, angels disagreeing? Will this ancient country survive the battle between apostates and fundamentalists? I wonder if the new regime, secularism, inclusivity, will impale itself, as did the caliphate, on compromise.

F

Of course, I am the voice of Güzel's father. We all have our parts to play.

Güzel knows that Mad's parents are dead. He forgot to remember that she hasn't yet learned the lesson about here and the sweet beyond; that life energy flows back and forth, conversations continue. She can still finish the business if she wishes. "If" is a strange word. Of course she wishes. Unfinished business is what her life is about. She may not believe in such things, but there are dying people who are willing to memorize messages for the dead. This service is a comfort to some, but unnecessary. The dead know what mortals are thinking. Of course they do. Mortals are predictable and their thoughts run in repetitious patterns. The trick is willing a negative pattern to change, re-programming.

Mad has noticed the birthmark. I think that is a lovely touch, reassurance of Güzel's mortality. He told her my Turkish name. I wonder if she is connecting the dots? She is, after all, here to re-boot her mind, although Iman, now flying from country to country in an airplane loaned to her by the American Secretary of State, is interfering with her thought patterns.

MOTHER SUPERIOR

I read on the Internet that a young female page in the House of Commons interrupted the throne speech after the Conservatives won their forty percent majority with a sign saying the Prime Minister must be stopped. STOP HARPER. In America that would mean "terminate with prejudice," uzis blazing, the way bin Laden was "brought to justice." But in Canada it implies "make accountable" or "keep honest," a process involving plea, petition and peaceful protest. Not as effective as termination, not as clean, but just. Way to go, former page.

I am proud of that young woman and reminded that in Canada we still have the luxury of complaint. The audacious page lost her job, but in many parts of the world she would have lost her head. The people I meet in Turkey whisper about fundamentalism. They fear change, the very thing their experiment with secularism has inspired in their Arab neighbours, but many feel powerless to protect the freedoms they have inherited. There is more in the newspapers about soccer than the Arab Spring, the murder of Osama bin Laden or the rape of Iman.

My mother used to call me a squeaky wheel, but how else are you going to get oil? Squeak and ye shall find. *Petitions, not pistols* is so Canadian.

Who should I write to to complain about the eels in the Gorge? That was my big concern the summer of Coon and me, before he vanished in the crack between summer and fall. Since I was used to sending whining letters to companies with imperfect products and getting freebies – some of them rip-ons and some of them treats like candy bars – and getting abject apologies in return, I thought there should be someone who would listen to me. I immediately thought of God. Coon had even less of a relationship with God than I did and neither of us had any idea how to address a letter to him.

Then there was the matter of what it would say. How does one address God? Do we start with Dear God or Our Father, or do we take a firmer tone? "God, this is not permissible. Clean up your act, or else." Maybe a venal pitch is necessary. How about this offer of a bribe, and I admit I would not have had a clue back then, "God, I'm willing to give you a hand release if you'll just make sure the Gorge is safe to swim in." Would he or she have heard that? There are many people addressing the higher power every day, something I have learned since I joined Al-Anon. So what is the best approach: prayer, song, or angry letters?

The people I know who have let Jesus into their hearts say God is everywhere and knows everything and everyone. I have absolutely no reason to believe this person or thing has ever noticed me. If it had, then my father and mother would have been left alone in their semi-happy domestic life until the four score and ten were used up, and then allowed to wither away like the leaves on the chestnut tree on our boulevard. That would have been natural. Instead, I got stuck with a big mess no kid should have to clean up. There is not much I could do about a dead dad and an alcoholic mum without help from somewhere. I was not about to become a team person. No one picked me for teams, not even God.

Around the middle of August, just when I had Coon feeling confident in the water, the eels moved in. At first I only saw one or two, but then they came in schools, thousands of them. One hot day I woke up at noon from a horrible deep sleep and my bed was just teeming with eels. They were in my mouth and ears and even got inside my pajamas.

I wrote to the mayor. My mother referred to the mayor as the boss of the city and I thought he would be flattered. She told me that whenever a policeman stopped me I should address him as "Sergeant" because ordinary cops were not sergeants. Most policemen were corporals who wanted to be sergeants and would be chuffed by the promotion.

Dear Boss,

Eels have invaded the Selkirk Gorge. Now eels can't vote, so you shouldn't be on their side. Prisoners can't vote either. Since you're a law and order guy and criminals would never vote for you, prison is the best place for them. I suggest you find a way of putting the eels in jail, or I won't be voting for you either.

Yours Truly,

Mother Turka.

I hoped the mayor followed my logic. In case he didn't, I sent carbon copies to all the aldermen, but this time I left off sending my letter to the newspaper. My letter was signed "Mother" and not "Madeleine" because I had the bright idea he might think I was a Mother Superior with God on my side.

That, I told myself, while I licked and sealed the envelope, was a stroke of brilliance.

Coon and I stayed awake until morning many times, but the night I'll never forget is the evening of the first aurora borealis. We were sitting outside the cave, choking on a couple of cigarettes I had stolen from the box beside Stella's bed when the northern sky lit up. Inside the shimmering arc, spumes of green florescence flared and faded. Coon and I were mesmerized by this great living stage with its faint radio noises. I wondered if my daddy lived inside that huge green scrim and wondered if he was trying to send me a message. My chest ached and I circled the feeling with both arms. It didn't matter. I knew he was there. I understood and was comforted.

The next day, by a strange coincidence, I got an answer from the mayor.

Dear Mother Superior,

Thank you for drawing the eel situation to my attention. Heretofore, we hadn't considered them a problem. Have you considered that you might be experiencing a religious crisis? Since the eel migration is an act of God, I would respectfully suggest that you pray for a solution to your difficulty. Consider swimming with eels an act of faith, Mother. Perhaps in a perfect world, nuns and eels will reconcile and once again co-habit the ocean. I am one of those who believe that all life comes from the sea. It could be the eels, or the idea of eels, are inviting you to communion.

If my reply is unsatisfactory to you, please contact the Department of Fisheries.

Yours, etc.

Mayor Thomas Barton.

What the hell did that mean? Is that how the mayor got rid of problems he didn't want to deal with, by passing them off as hallucinations? I saw the eels. Perhaps he was put off by my threatening tone. Maybe he was raised by nuns and had a grudge. I've had lots of clients who've been abused by Sisters of the Child Jesus. I've heard stories of paddlings, sexual touching, withholding of food, forced feeding of lumpy potatoes and standing in the rain in pajamas. Sadly, their former victims often out-nun the nuns when it comes to perverse adult behaviour. That's when I get them for unholy healing.

Coon and I learned to live with the eels. I even went so far as to eat one to prove my courage to him. We made a fire on the beach and I caught a hideous creature with a net I'd made with a coat hanger and one of Stella's dance dresses. The eel wasn't that bad. I've heard that they are sacred in parts of Italy. I washed it down with a half bottle of sherry I found in the liquor cupboard. Stella didn't drink sherry. My dad must have had the bottle around for church ladies and priests, and they didn't come any more. Coon just watched.

I moved all my candy to the cave. Lying on my back, watching the Northern Lights and shooting stars with an Oh Henry in my hand was my personal heaven. I started by licking off the chocolate and then eating one nut at a time until I got to the caramel centre. Coon demolished the bars. I'm surprised he removed the wrappers. Once, when I took him a bunch of bananas he ate them skin and all. Coon ate the skins on everything – fish, potatoes, apples and bananas – all of it.

I trusted Coon with my candy stash because his cave was my cave, as my father used to say in his adopted second language. Building up provisions was the first step to moving out. Even though I knew I couldn't really leave Stella, it felt good to have a place of my own. What if she let a cigarette fall down the crack in her chair, or if it caught in a curtain or the carpet or in her bed, and the house burned down? Then we would have had no place to go but the cave. I could take her there and Coon and I could look after her. When the fire was lit, she could watch shadows flare on the wall instead of the TV set.

When I got home the night I'd carried the last load of provisions to the cave, Stella was watching *You Were Never Lovelier*, with Fred Astaire and Rita Hayworth. Instead of lying back in the Easyboy, she was leaning forward, singing along, with her arms raised up as if she had them around Fred. I remembered sneaking out of bed to watch her dancing in the living room with Daddy, her body molded to his, her mouth next to his ear whispering the words to "Paper Doll" or "Unchained Melody." She was still doing it, only Fred was Daddy and Rita was her.

"Tell me about Rita," I said, snuggling in beside her.

"Shhhh," Stella whispered. It was almost over.

When Fred and Rita disappeared in a soft focus of glitter and net, she ran her fingers through my hair. I loved it when she did that. Stella could put me to sleep by just scratching my back or rubbing my temples. I haven't been able to find anyone else who will do that and, prior to my recent windfall, couldn't afford to hire my own masseur.

"Tell me," I insisted. It was the middle of the night and my eyelids were dropping.

"Rita was a husky little girl, just like you, but she could dance. Boy, could she dance."

"And she danced off all her jiggly bits, right?"

"It wasn't bits, Mother. It was baby fat."

"Whatever," I said and yawned, and the ceramic panther on top of the television set blinked his green glass eye. He winked at me. Stella was full of crap and he knew it.

"Her name wasn't Rita then. She changed it when she became a movie star. What will we call you when you grow up?"

"Anything but 'Mother.'"

"That was your daddy's idea."

"I know."

"Rita got into the movies because she could dance. She dyed her brown hair red. See, you don't even have to do that. Your hair is already the right colour."

That was an exaggeration. My hair has red *highlights*, and that is nowhere near flaming red like Rita Hayworth's.

"Some day you will be famous. You will fly off to Hollywood or New York City on a magic carpet and you'll take your old mum with you, because you're a good kid. When you have your own children, I'll take care of them so you can go off and walk the red carpet with guys like Cary Grant and Fred Astaire. Just make sure you say goodnight to your old mother when you're on television, just like Carol Burnett."

"Carol is saying good night to her grandmother, Stella. Her mum is a drunk."

I didn't believe her fairy tales for one minute, but I still liked hearing them. Red carpets, ha. More likely, I'd be taking a hike into the woods and meeting up with a wicked old witch who would throw me straight into her oven, because I was already chunky enough to make a great Wiccan dinner.

"Rita has it all. She's a star. She married an Arab prince and has two beautiful daughters. The world is her oyster."

"Do Arabs eat oysters, Stella? Do oysters grow in the desert?"

"Of course, they do. King Farouk died when he ate too many. His stomach exploded right thorough his dress shirt."

"Well, maybe they shouldn't then." Stella didn't know everything but there were times when she thought she did. I was in no danger of believing her, any more than I believed my father came back to dance with her.

"People used to mistake your daddy and me for Fred and Ginger. He was a wonderful dancer. When I was a kid on the farm, I watched eagles teach their babies to fly. The trick was to catch an updraught of air and ride on it. Hot air rises, Mother. Your daddy was my hot air balloon."

"Like pretending to be an Arab prince, you mean?"

I remembered him singing "The Sheik of Araby."

"Your father was not an Arab." She said A-rab. "He was a Tuscan Turk, descended from the Etruscans. He was a big talker, and lots of it was fairy tale, but he sure could dance. Maybe one day, you'll find some hot air to ride on."

In my mind, I still rode my father's feet to bed every night while he sang to me. "Relax your mind," he used to say. "Let your body hear the music." Stella had no proverbs to give me, but she did blow on my face so I could breath in the smell of smoke and gin and the lovely feelings like flowers planted deep inside her. I was almost asleep and she was still petting my head.

"I love you, little Mother. I wish I could be happier for you."

"I wish you could too," I said, and I meant it with all my heart.

In a movie magazine, I read that Fred said Ginger stepped on his feet.

BYZANTINE LATRINE

I can't help obsessing about the women in *hajibs*. At night I lie in bed and imagine what it would feel like to be wearing a shroud in summer. *Well,* I said to myself, *they're oven-ready. Just pop them in the ground when they expire of grief or the heat.* This got me thinking about Pamuk's headscarf girls.

I know that among those who believe it is instinctive to cover our heads before God – even the monkeys do it, making hats with their hands – but would God want us to suffer in this way? I doubt it – not a god that fits any definition I can find or think up myself.

What would I die for? It is easy to say I would jump in front of a car to push a child out of the way. Or would I? Isn't the first reaction to impending tragedy a kind of paralysis? We move as if in dreams toward a foregone conclusion.

Is this entire country paralyzed when it hears that young Anatolian women are hanging themselves rather than bringing shame to their families and their religion by going bareheaded or falling in love with infidels? Why are these people burying their children? What a waste of a mother's love. Practically speaking, what a waste of food.

If the rumours coming out of Kurdistan are true, these girls are not true suicides. It is their fathers and brothers who are encouraging them to tie ropes around their necks or jump off bridges. Perhaps their loving family members kick away the chairs or help them over the rails in their cumbersome attire.

And what about their mothers? Do the mothers close their eyes to all this? I close my eyes and see the hand of an African mother holding the razor she will use to circumcise her daughter, causing her a lifetime of suffering and perhaps even death. I see Chinese mothers breaking the tiny bones in their daughters' feet to deform them for the sake of some cursed standard of beauty; golden lilies, my ass.

Does our deranged species deserve to inherit the Earth?

Who in their right mind would send a kid off to war and throw away time spent walking the floor with a crying infant, telling her stories, teaching her to read and write, or to swim? Twenty-odd years of careful nurturing down the toilet; just like that. It is unthinkable.

Is that why Pamuk's God is as silent as snow, because he or she is aghast, speechless before the desecration of human life, the interruption of bees?

I have to admit I have a thing about draperies and suffocation. Every time I walked into my mother's house with its closed curtains and the smells of gin and cigarettes, I saw death. I see death on the streets of Istanbul, those women and girls with their curtains drawn. They are the living dead. No wonder Turkey is in quiet turmoil. No wonder the Earth is dizzy on its axis of evil.

What keeps me moving is knowing that Iman's mother fought back, defending her daughter on television. She is the real Arab Spring.

◦෴◦

I wonder how Turks endure the heat, as we drive east from Izmir, ancient Smyra. Everywhere I look, there are people working like the mad dogs and Englishmen in that Noel Coward song my father played until the grooves on the record wore out. Farmers are actually burning their fields, reducing the stubble from harvested crops to ashes so they can plant again. The effort must be excruciating in the summer heat. There must be a point where human blood actually does boil. I must find out what that would be.

When we arrive at Sardis, a truck filled with bottles of water pulls up at the same time as a tourist bus. I wonder what parched Romans did on a day like this when they were constructing these buildings? At the moment we are fighting more wars over oil, but what is oil compared to water? We will get back to that battle. I am sure I will see the day when American troops march into Canada to take over our water supplies. Why wouldn't they? It's entirely in character. Our weapons of mass destruction are the comedians who see through their puerile logic. Hopefully, fully armed Americans practicing ultimate population control, will kill each other off before the day comes when we become the butt of the joke.

Because I wanted to stay in the moment and remember only what my memory selected today, I left my camera in Izmir. Now I wish I had at least brought a sketchbook to record the textures in the buildings, the exquisite tiles and mosaics that pre-date the artisanship in which the Muslims take such pride. I am astonished by the presence of a synagogue in this Roman community of polytheists. When did people become so exclusive, and why?

Perhaps I will make a Turkish garden, with a grape arbor and a mosaic floor. I am getting old enough to take gardening seriously. Maybe I followed my father here just to hear Voltaire.

"It is beautiful," I say, standing on what remains of a mosaic floor.

"This is the meaning of life," my companion asserts. "Broken pieces side by side, making a whole picture."

"You are a poet, Güzel."

"We are all poets if we allow ourselves. It is in our nature to select and arrange."

Güzel draws my attention to a sign in English over what appears to be a horizontal stone bench with indentations. The notice says BYZANTINE LATRINE. It must be a joke. I am astonished. I can hardly say toilet words in public and I thought the Turks were modest to the extreme. Hasn't Güzel been warning me at every opportunity to cover up and turn down the volume?

"It's not about sexuality. It's about cleanliness," he says, as we cross the road to an outdoor restaurant snuggling in an oasis of trees and running water. There is a stream beside the truck stop café, which has been diverted into a waterfall where drivers can pass through and wash the dust off their cars.

"Yes, I know. The Romans had lovely toilets. The Turks have beautiful *tuvalets*."

While Güzel attends to nature, I sink down on a carpet-covered bench with soft cushions, order *çay* and hold up two fingers for the Kurdish woman rolling huge pancakes on a large, slightly rounded stone, which she then fills with cheese and bakes in a stone oven. We would like two. She looks surprised.

"I want to speak into the tape recorder," I tell Güzel when he comes to the low table and sits across from me.

"Of course."

"I am a typical mid-twentieth-century North American," I begin, "and I have no roots. I came to Turkey because the people in this country, even if they don't know where they are going, know where they come from. They know how to dress and what is healthy to eat. They are what they are and understand how they should behave." I pause when the pancakes arrive; they are delicious.

"In my country, we place a lot of importance on pedigree. People spend a lot of money, for example, acquiring purebred dogs, as if that meant something. I haven't seen a single purebred dog in Turkey. They all seem to be mongrels. Dogs and cats appear to be the street people of Turkey.

"That's not what I want to talk about, though. I want to talk about toilets. Before I came to this country I was advised to bring my own toilet paper, *tuvalet kağıdı yok.* I like the way that sounds, the consonants cresting like waves in water music, or flushes. There is no toilet paper. Here is the difference between my country and yours. In my country, people joke about using the pages from books for *tuvalet kağıdı.* Can you imagine anyone wiping their asses on sacred text in Turkey?

"I filled my luggage with paper, books to read, tissues to wipe my bottom and blow my nose. It was unnecessary. Even though English books are expensive and hard to find, there is so much else to engage the eye; and the toilets are so beautifully appointed. I want to commend you on your toilets, especially the little device.

"At first I didn't understand what the device was for. It terrified me. Was it some sort of nannycam for the bum, a sneaky surveillance device stashed in the least likely of hiding places? I was afraid to use the toilet when I first arrived here for fear of insulting Turkishness, desecrating the device with my body waste or, at the very least, electrocuting myself by creating an electron path between myself and it, whatever 'it' is.

"Now I understand. The device is meant for washing the derrière. I have found that those cunning little taps on the wall activate the device, which then gives forth a pleasant stream of water. How evolved. North America has a long way to go before it begins to approach such ingenuity.

"Even the old-fashioned toilets with footprints and holes in the floor have devices. I was fooling with one just yesterday, at the mosque in the Konak market. I was properly dressed, shirt, shoes, skirt, borrowed coat, scarf. It was quite a business doing my business. How do Muslim women have sex and babies and go the bathroom without occasionally "compromising" their clothing. I'm not sure I could do it.

"While I squatted, holding up my skirts, enjoying the sound of my stream on an unbearably hot day, I mused on such things. What if my father's family had stayed in Turkey and converted to Islam in, say, the seventh or eighth century? Would I now be wandering around in three layers of clothing, wondering what humiliation might visit me in a public toilet?

"Just as I broke off a modest piece of *tuvalet kağıdı*, a brilliant circle of light came rolling over the tiles toward me. Was it enlightenment, some fragment of divinity? Cautiously, I reached out and touched the object when it had stopped spinning. I picked it up. It was a diamond ring.

"What a strange thing to befall me, albeit in a mosque, where miracles are just as much a possibility as they would be in a synagogue or a cathedral. I immediately thought of my mother's lost ring. Were the chicken gods returning it to me in a Turkish toilet? I put it on."

"Are you finished?"

"Yes," I say, turn off the recorder and stand up. I suppose I could have spoken directly to him.

"Can you tell the difference between Kurdish Christian women and Muslim women?" he asks.

"No."

"It's how they wear headscarves, the only difference."

The water in the car shower is beyond relief. I raise my arms and turn myself around and around. I don't care if the Turkish truck drivers lounging in the shade are surprised or amused. I don't care if my nipples show through my wet dress. The ring on my left hand sparkles in the sunlight. I know it. Iman is a married woman. Safe?

"What did you do with the alleged diamond?" he inquires, as if it might have been imaginary or fake.

"I found its owner," I answer.

COON'S BOTTLE TREE

The world is full of beautiful bottles. My mother chose the square-shouldered lady filled with forgetfulness, but I don't want to forget. I like the blue bottles best. My African client, Mr. Magawe, told me that blue glass is lucky. Blue bottles sing like the sea. When I listen to them, I hear dolphins searching the ocean for relatives, waves rhyming on the beach, and slaves rowing in unison. "How is that lucky?" I asked Mr. Magawe, and because he answers questions with questions, he asked, "Why not?" Doesn't luck change?

Mine never has. I still sleep in the same bed in the same room in the same house in the same neighbourhood where I was born in the middle of the twentieth century. Sometimes I think I am afraid to leave in case I might miss something, or maybe like Istanbul, perched between Asia Minor and Europe, my room might be a fulcrum between heaven and hell, past and present.

That might be the message from my father, his voice captured in the bottles with those of all the unhappy spirits who hang around after their time is up.

My mother said that was where I got Coon. Like a genie, he came out of one of my bottles. She never believed in him, even after I took her to see the bottle tree we made outside his cave.

Stella huffed and puffed but I held her hand and dragged her up the hill behind me. My mother was rarely sober enough to greet the sun, so this was a big day. I wanted to make it even bigger by showing her the secret world I had hidden from her all summer. What the heck?

"I'm teaching him to read," I squeezed out between breaths. "He's an orphan." I snuck a look at her to see if the word registered, but she just puffed along in her pink quilted housecoat and fluffy slippers, her eyes on the ground, as if a hand, maybe my father's or that of his other partner, might reach up and take her to dance in the underworld.

We stopped in front of the cave. I pointed and Stella looked up at Coon's beautiful arbutus, festooned with bottles and ribbons. Her eyes must have hurt looking at the light, but she walked all around the tree, catching every angle of the sun in its branches.

"*You* made it, Mother. It's got you written all over it."

"How come?" I asked her. How the hell could she tell what did or did not have my name written on it? She had been looking at me through the end of a bottle for more than a thousand nights. This day, however, Stella was sober and I wanted a straight answer. This was our moment. She'd waited up for me, all the way to morning. I was so happy to see her sitting in her chair actually missing me, actually asking the question *I'd* been waiting to hear, "Where were you, young lady?" that I told her about Coon. When I finished, she said I'd been with the fairies and come back telling lies.

"It's all blue bottles."

I whistled, but Coon wasn't there. He must have been off foraging. I took her inside the cave and showed her his bed and his fire and the provisions he'd gathered. "You see," I said. "He's real. This is where he lives. That bottle tree you saw outside is his. He's waiting to hear from his mother who died in a terrible accident. She was smeared all over the road, like peanut butter."

"Who told you that?"

"He did."

"That's a lie. No real kid would say that about his mother. That's a joke. Everything you say comes out of books or your cockamamie brain, Mother."

"You're a liar." I tried to yell louder than crying because I was so ashamed of my tears. She didn't deserve to hurt my feelings. "And you're a terrible mother. I'm not supposed to even *know* your name. Hardly any of the kids at school know their mother's names. They're real mothers and they don't embarrass their kids by being drunk and dancing to music from the Stone Age. Their mothers dance to the Rolling Stones and they drink real coffee, not that crap in a jar."

Stella ran down the hill and I ran after her screaming, "Stella. Stella. Stella!" I hated her. "No wonder my daddy left us. You are so butt ugly, you scared him to death!"

I threw that word "ugly" all the way down the hill. It hit our fence and I watched it turn around and smack her right in the face. I know that happened because I saw the ugly wound.

"And he got married to Coon's mum in Heaven." My *coup de grâce.*

I sat down in the grass where she'd collapsed in a bloody, sweaty heap and started crying too. Out of the corner of my eye

I could see the neighbours were getting up to start a new day. First, their curtains moved and then, when they got braver and more curious, I saw their faces in the windows. Some of them even came outside in their pajamas to get a better look.

Somehow I got Stella into the house. She was a dead weight. I wondered if my dad ever felt that way. I could imagine him saying, "Stella is a heavy woman." Whenever I heard that song "Sixteen Tons," I thought of her. I thought of my dad dragging her around the dance floor the way that Jesus freak from the halfway house carries his big heavy cross through town on Good Friday, the way Fred schlepped Ginger.

"I'm sorry, Stella," I gasped between sobs. "I don't know what got into me. Maybe I need more sleep."

"We both miss your dad," Stella sniffed, her eyes red from crying, while she lined up those green coke glasses she likes on the wicker tray. She sure could move quickly when she wanted to. I watched her pour what my dad used to call "a big hook of gin," then two ice cubes and a splash of tonic in each glass. With her "mother's tea" poured in advance, she was all set for *The Edge of Night*.

Stella had her cry and that was that. She went back to her juniper berries of forgetfulness and turned on the TV set. The moment was past. Alone again, I decided I had to fix things once and for all. If one bottle tree wasn't enough spiritual power to protect my family, then I was going to have a whole yard full of bottle trees. I went right down to Safeway and got myself a shopping cart. Coon and I were in the bottle business.

We hunted by night, catting around with hungry strays in alleys, vacant lots and garbage cans. "Seek and ye shall find," the Bible says, and I can witness to the wealth of bottles of every shape and colour in the backyards of this world. It didn't take long to load the grocery cart, and as soon as it was full we took it back to our yard and hung the bottles on the trees – all of them – the fruit trees, the evergreens and the maples. Sometimes we mixed up the colours and sometimes we went for just one. We decorated the peach tree with yellow and orange glass. It looked so pretty when the sun shone through those bottles.

Even after Coon, I kept taking care of my song trees. Sometimes a bottle smashed to the ground. Sometimes the colour faded and the bottle didn't capture the light any more. I had acquired a taste for collecting. Finding them had become some kind of compulsion. I am never so happy as when I am wheeling my rusty cart through the empty streets at 3 a.m., keeping my eyes open for that special glass that calls out to me in the moonlight.

The problem is, I found so many bottles I had to find a place to keep them. My big number one and number two rules have always been: DO NOT USE HOUSE BOTTLES and DO NOT TAKE FOUND BOTTLES INTO THE HOUSE. As far as I was concerned, our home was like those crime scenes with yellow tape around them. It was contaminated by sadness and inhabited by the spirits that took my mother away from me. There was not one liquor bottle on any of my trees.

Because of my daddy's genes, I turned out to be a very tall girl and, by virtue of my experience in taking care of Stella, I had what horse people call "soft hands." Masseuses and hairdressers require strength, but also what I call kindness in the hands. For some souls, we are the only ones who touch them. My first job was a private request from an old man whose house I cleaned, thanks to an ad posted on the board down at

Jung's grocery store. One thing led to another and I eventually started giving my client a hand release for an extra five bucks.

If someone were to ask me whether I preferred housecleaning or personal services, I would be hard pressed to give an answer. There is a lot of pride in all of my work. I like to see a clean house that smells fresh and has vacuum lines in the carpet. I hate to see people walk over a fresh carpet. There is also a lot of satisfaction in giving satisfaction. I've been told there is nothing more beautiful than the smile on the face of a woman who has just given birth, but I'd be willing to bet her old grandmother in the rest home looks just as happy when she gets her personal care.

Both of my jobs are low overhead. I just have to get to work and I have two good legs and a bicycle for that. Sometimes I take the bus, but only when it's raining hard. That's one of the good things about living in Victoria. There is no place that is too far away. My clients must have their own cleaning gear and all I take for the extra touch is a bottle of Astroglide lubricant and surgical gloves.

My rest home services are discreet. All my clients have private rooms with doors that lock. The home clients are another story. Some of them have privacy issues. When I started my business, Stella was still living at home. I couldn't take them home to her. There was no way I could keep up with her untidiness and I didn't even try, even after I became a professional housecleaner. No question about it, I needed a place to store bottles and take care of private clients. One day when I was walking along Esquimalt Road I saw a sign for a storage locker.

I rented a private room, a ten-by-ten foot locker. I had the only key. The locker opens on the street and is available twenty-four hours a day. My clients can access it any time they want. They just have to book an appointment and use discretion. First, I got some two-by-fours and made shelves for my treasures, which I laid down on their sides according to size and colour. The bottles make a pretty wall and they also provide insulation. When I had my shelves, I went to yard sales and found a high table and stepladder, a heater, a worn Turkish carpet and a floor lamp. I covered the table with a foamy and a quilt from home. Not only was I *in* business, I had a *place* of business. In no time at all, I had enough referred customers to pay for the locker.

Before I had a business address, I charged five dollars for a hand release. Eventually I charged ten and nobody complained. Then I went up to twenty. That's for the first hour, and I charge extra for socializing afterward. The funny thing is, I had been under the impression that using a storage locker for something other than storage was all my idea. It wasn't too long before I realized I had rented myself a community. My nocturnal neighbours include a pair of hookers, a few street people who rent a locker for safe sleeping, and a headbanger band that practices at night. They are noisy, but so are my clients. Over the years we have shared the same rhythm, a few bottles of wine, and many cups of instant soup. From time to time I choose a bottle from my collection to take home to my trees, but mostly I leave them there because they hold onto the passionate exhalations of my customers.

I've only had one client give me anxiety. She was an eighty-nine-year-old widow in need of regular loving touch. Mrs. Willoughby visited once a week, every Friday after she had her hair done. When I asked her why she came to me with her fresh coiffure, she told me her husband liked her to look nice.

He didn't want to see her in curlers or wearing face cream. Mrs. W. was one of the few people I saw in the daytime, and I made the exception because she was afraid to go out at night. Her hair appointment was at 10 a.m. and, at 11.50 on the dot, a taxi delivered her to my locker. She told me she had informed the driver that she was checking up on her dead husband's possessions, which she had moved out of the house and into the locker on the other side of the band's after he went to spirit because it made her sad to live with his suits and collection of brass instruments.

"Brass?" I asked.

"Well, yes," she said. "He practiced in the garage."

Mrs. Willoughby chatted with her husband while I took her to bliss. I wondered if she had been one of those ladies who talk all the way through sex and drive their husbands crazy. I know about that because the husbands tell me personal things. So do wives. Mrs. W. cried out his name and, when she did, her voice was like a young girl's. Her husband Wilbur lives in my bottles and I have a sacred obligation to him.

On her ninetieth birthday, Mrs. Willoughby made a special appointment. It was not on a Friday at 11.50 a.m. She came just before midnight on a Thursday.

"Happy birthday," I said. "Is your cabby waiting?"

"I walked," she told me. "It's only three blocks. I didn't want the driver to ask me why I was out so late and think I was dithering," she laughed.

"I suppose he would," I said. "I have a special treat for you." I had bought a bottle of sherry and two little marzipan tarts they sell for half price at Patisserie Danielle after four o'clock. After helping her to sit up on the table, I poured the sherry in two of my mother's crystal wedding glasses. Then I lit the candle on her cake and banged on the wall between my locker and the headbangers' rehearsal space. The boys in the band played "Happy Birthday" and she blew out her candle and wished. Mrs. Willoughby and I clinked glasses. "To life," I said, and we drank.

While I helped Mrs. Willoughby, she told me about her wedding, which had been on her twenty-first birthday. She'd met her husband at church. They both sang in the choir. When they got married, the choir sang "Praise My Soul Oh King of Heaven." Mrs. Willoughby sang it for me, and her voice was steady and true.

"When you sing," I said, "you sound like a girl."

"I *am* a girl," she assured me and closed her eyes.

After telling me about her wedding dress and the brides-maids' dresses, Mrs. Willoughby described her wedding night. She had not been disappointed, she said. Wilbur was a very thoughtful husband. I remembered the story one of my customers told me about making her tongue-tied husband have his tongue surgically cut so he could pleasure her orally. I wondered if Wilbur Willoughby did things like that.

Right in the middle of her description of her first climax, Grace Willoughby called out her husband's name with so much force I nearly fell back from the table. In the near dark, I could hear my bottles sucking in Wilbur. The headbangers heard it too. They stopped playing. Then, all there was left to hear was my own heart.

"Mrs. Willoughby," I said at last. "Grace?" But Grace had gone to Glory Land and stayed there.

I sat in the dark, wondering what I was going to do with my adorable widow. It wouldn't look good if she was found in my locker. That was sure to happen sooner or later. Everything gets found out in the end. I learned that the summer of Coon. The storage lockers are cold, but they are not mortuaries.

Luckily, Mrs. Willoughby had her house keys and a Care Card with her address on it in her purse. She'd been carrying twenty-seven dollars and forty-two cents in cash. I didn't take the cash for her last visit, but I did finish her package of Werther's toffee while I was deciding how to lose Grace. By the time the last candy melted in my mouth, I had made my decision.

The guys in the band were surprised to see me. I begged, and, I have to admit, I cried; and they agreed to help. There were six of them; just enough to provide Mrs. Willoughby's earthly remains with a nice escort home. The trombonist who carried her fireman-style up her front stairs, much the same way that Wilbur had carried her to bed all those years ago, said she was as light as a feather.

THE CESME HAMAM

"I think of them as onions," I say to Hannah, the younger and more overtly serious of the Sweet Papa Lowdown daughters. Hannah thinks I am too critical of the Muslim women who wear layers of clothing in this obscenely hot weather while the men and young children enjoy the relative freedom of summer clothing. "Maybe they are nearer to God, like the onion-shaped domes in their mosques. They sure do *smell* like onions."

Hannah frowns. I am reading her mind. She is clearly not happy with my flippant criticism. How can I come to this country and pass judgment? How dare I intrude with my own definition of freedom? Haven't Muslim women expressed their happiness with the anonymity of a uniform?

"You don't see any of them smiling, do you, Hannah? They are miserably hot, and their eyes are dead."

"How can you tell whether they are smiling or not when their mouths are covered?" She pulls out of her slumped "think" posture, looking me full in the face.

"Eyes laugh too. I'll buy you lunch if you can make one of the girls smile." I assign her a girl because teenagers are tribal.

Her sister Naomi laughs. Naomi knows I have challenged Hannah to stand up straight, a posture she folds up with her self-esteem.

"Will you buy mine as well?" she asks. Naomi could charm a mouse out of a cheese cupboard.

We are walking down the main street of Cesme, drinking water and avoiding the leading questions that will drag us into uncomfortable situations with shop owners. "Are you Canadian?" "Can I show you some beautiful Turkish carpets?" "Would you like a cup of çay?" The dark interiors of their places of business unsettle the girls, who have heard my cautionary stories of Istanbul. I feel protective of them because, if I were normal instead of the adult child of older parents, one of them an alcoholic, I might have gone out and grabbed a real life for myself and had teenaged daughters of my own.

Even as a mature woman I still have the power and the fear of my own sexuality, men leering from cars, and men whistling when I walk past their workplaces.

"I've talked to Muslim girls at home and they say they like being covered. Those girls are free to be themselves. They don't have to put up with men staring at them the way we do. I don't know why you have to feel sorry for them." Naomi, who is wearing a low-cut tank top and shorts, agrees with her sister.

"It isn't a hundred degrees in the shade at home," I say.

"The *hajib* is protection," Hannah retorts.

"Did it protect Iman al-Obeidi from being raped and beaten?" I ask.

We have arrived at a Muslim "coat store." Dozens of the ugly shapes sulk on racks in the cavernous shop while a half dozen are buttoned on street dummies as still and stiff as the headscarf girls who hang themselves.

"Let's try some on," Naomi suggests. First we buy scarves and tie them around our heads. Then we put on the death-coats, buttoning them up to the neck. We are a glum of uninspired shoppers, but the shop girl tolerates us. Business is business.

"I'm roasting," Hannah complains.

"Exactly."

Naomi gives her camera to the shop girl who good-humouredly takes some photos, and seems happy when we purchase our scarves.

"She smiled," Hannah says as we leave. I guess I *will* be buying lunch.

"What," I ask, attacking my *tavuk sis* with a fork, "would these toe-tapping Muslim ladies do if they knew what the lyrics in Papa's blues songs really meant? Would they smile at 'jelly roll' or 'big banana' or would they have their husbands cut off the musicians' heads in the public square?"

"Everyone likes jelly roll," wise Hannah remarks, even though she has never tried it. I will ask Güzel. He might even offer me some.

❦

While we ate, sunbathed and slept in the cabana this afternoon, Güzel and I traded stories. I told him that my father had assumed an Italian identity after serving in Sicily during World War Two. Apparently he had enjoyed being a sex tourist at war. My father's family was from Tuscany. Maybe there was genetic recognition in his attraction to Mediterranean women, especially the film stars of the Fifties and Sixties. I am only one degree removed from the soldier who hungered in the killing fields of Calabria.

Now there is evidence that the Etruscans immigrated to Italy from Smyrna during a terrible famine in pre-Christian times. The population was forced to draw lots. Half of them had to leave or they would all starve. My mother said she knew he was a Turk. I have no idea whether this is true or not.

"I am from Izmir," Güzel says, while we are sweating in the Cesme *hamam*. In spite of the hot weather, I was determined to have a Turkish bath. Mind over matter; it is a test to see if I can take what I dish out, hands on. I have never had a massage. We are the only ones here. In this *hamam* there is no separation of men and women. I pick up a towel and a sarong in the common changing room. Despite the fact that I want Güzel to see me naked, I am careful changing into my cotton wrap.

"Maybe we are related," I say, turning so that I am lying on my stomach on the sweating platform in the centre of the steam bath.

Güzel laughs and I wonder about the incest taboos in Islam but do not say anything because that would presume intimacy.

The slab is marble and, since there is nothing to grab onto, my fingers slip on the damp surface.

"I am nervous," I say. "I am not used to being touched."

"But you touch people all the time."

"It's not the same thing. I give the healing touch. No one touches me. My father used to tickle me. It made me nervous."

"That was a long time ago."

"Yes, I'm trying to get over it. I have lots of phobias. I like to take pictures, but I'm shy about being photographed."

"Is it about power?"

"Maybe. I don't know. I do know there is a missing piece."

"I hope you will find it."

"I will. Meanwhile, I do get a lot of satisfaction from my job."

"Do you find it hard to work with old people?" he asks, his voice choking on the steam.

"Why?"

"It must be sad. I understand it is the North American custom to abandon elders. Surely, they are unhappy."

"That's true, but my vocation is to give them back their joy."

"How do you do that?"

"I play music. I read to them. I make beautiful food." I hesitate. "I give them a massage."

"Relax and enjoy it," he says as Mahmoud, the masseur, begins to scrub my legs with a loofah and I feel the dead skin sloughing off.

"Yes. Sometimes the healer needs to heal herself. I just lost a very special client." I don't say that he left me the money that allowed me to take time off for travel. He might think I am a grifter.

"My patient married a younger woman in Las Vegas without telling his family. As soon as the ink was dry on the deed to her new house, she put him out. Even though he had just bought her a car, she made him take a bus to the airport. After that, he was depressed, wouldn't wear his glasses, his false teeth or his hearing aid. My client shut down, but he never gave up hoping that she would come and get him. He said she promised him sex in exchange for her house and the marriage, but she didn't keep her end of the bargain.

"My client's grief was heartbreaking. I couldn't bear the look of anticipation on his face when her letters demanding money arrived. He asked me to read them to him. I left out the abusive parts. Perhaps I shouldn't have because, even though she never visited him, he named her as his executor and as next of kin on his hospital admission papers. He put off dying so he could see her one last time. But she didn't come until it was time for the reading of his will. When he died, his real family couldn't claim his body and give him a respectful burial. She left him rotting in the morgue for two weeks while she ransacked his house and took off with his financial papers."

"That would never happen in my country."

"God bless your country, Güzel."

The masseur lightly slaps my shoulder and tells me to turn over. He has dipped what looks like a long pillowcase in soapy water and blown into it. Now he is covering my body with suds. It is the gentlest of massages. I close my eyes and enjoy the intimacy. Even though massage is my work, and I am used to the emotional reaction to touch, I am surprised by the feelings that surface. I think I am going to weep, for myself, for my father, for the poor old man who was weak enough to fall in love with a woman who didn't deserve him.

Ahhh. Mahmoud has discovered my vulnerable place. I have weak ankles. My feet are so happy I think they will sing. Someone speaks in my ear. I open my eyes and see the masseur with his face next to mine, his grin filled with gold while he also massages my feet and lower legs, a little Turkish joke I think. Güzel is lying on the other side of the platform, his face turned away from me.

"You have long arms, Mahmoud." I go along with the joke, whatever it is, as he pretends to be confused.

Mahmoud delivers me to the sinks, gives me a copper *hamam* bowl and leaves me to bathe myself in cool water.

"I feel clean," I say. "Even my brain."

When my friend joins me, we lie side by side, scrubbed, massaged, fresh as newborn babies. I ache to take his hand and wonder if he feels the same.

"Our friend, the comedian, didn't massage my chest and shoulders," I say.

"Turkish men are respectful."

Güzel and I carefully peel off the platform. We are modest. I put on my slippers and arrive at the door first.

"Güzel! It's locked!"

UNHOLY MATRIMONY

Brother, friend, or lover, I don't know why I needed Coon so badly the summer I turned the corner on adolescence. He was the only one who came close in every category. I talked to him, looked after him and adored him. I wanted to be a little wife, Mrs. Mother, to do the things my own mother had forgotten when she let herself drown in grief. At home, I kept my own room tidy and struggled with the rest of the house, but Coon's cave was whole, manageable, a house. Ours. I made a broom out of a cedar branch and dusted with the red polka dot handkerchief I'd used to cover my face when I robbed banks after breaking into neighbourhood games of cowboys and Indians.

One day, a hummingbird flew into our kitchen window and stunned itself. I picked it up and carried it to the cave where I cared for it tenderly, fed it sugar water through the dropper in a used-up medicine bottle. Within days, we had a mouse, a kitten, several tree frogs and a snake. They were all family – my second family, and Coon's only one.

There were times when I believed I would grow up and get married like the brides and grooms who rode in the back seats of cars covered with crepe paper streamers and horns honking every Saturday in summer. I went uninvited to church weddings and cried when the groom kissed the bride. I threw confetti. I cut their faces out of the photos in the free newspaper and replaced them with drawings of my own. These brides were tiny and happy. I kept growing taller.

My size is an advantage in my work. I can bear down on my clients, who like it when my big hands squeeze out the sadness they store in their bodies like tubes of toothpaste. It isn't just a one-way street. When I give pleasure, I feel it. Sure, some of them are demanding and cranky, some are filled up with flagrant ingratitude. Others laugh or cry when I find the places where memories sleep. Then they are grateful. Those feelings creep up my arms and find their way to my heart. I like my job.

These days, I have no desire to get married. I could give myself to a man and end up like Stella. What possible good would that do? I'd rather get used to loneliness than be assaulted by loss when I least expected or needed it. Most marriages end in divorce. In the ones that stay together, somebody dies first. Marriage is like having a dog or a canary. A person spends all that time and money on food and vet bills and tidying up, and ends up staring into a hole in the ground. Not me. I'm not taking any risks. I have a mortgage-free house. I get to eat what I want when I want, go to movies and buy a round-trip ticket to Seattle on the Victoria *Clipper* once a year.

I've lived by myself ever since checking Stella into a rest home on her seventieth birthday. I had to; the booze pickled her brain. She'd left water running in the bathtub and, after a window in her dementia allowed her to rediscover her love of cookery, forgot to turn off the stove. Every pot was ruined. She didn't even recognize me at the end. Her brain had drowned in ninety-proof.

When I took her out for walks in her wheelchair – the fresh air alternative to watching television – we visited shops. I knew from her rhapsodic descriptions of my daddy moving rocks and plants in the garden that she missed watching people at work. We spent hours standing in front of the counter at McDonald's watching the workers punch numbers, slap burgers into buns and scoop up fries. She liked watching barbers give haircuts and clerks pack groceries. Stella and I had quite an entertainment system worked out.

One afternoon I pushed her to the flower shop on Esquimalt Road to take her mind off a permanent wave in progress. The ladies who worked there were new Chinese immigrants and didn't speak much English. The florists ran about the shop, fussing with arrangements, while silent Stella made a surprisingly articulate speech about plants and Daddy and how she never had to buy flowers because he had something nice in the garden twelve months a year.

I didn't get it together to fix up his garden. By the time I'd survived childhood, I was working full time and caring for her. Gardening was the last thing on my list of things to do, but I knew Stella liked flowers. Once a week I bought her a bouquet at Jung's market, and she put them in the window just in case the neighbours had the idea that we didn't care about beautiful things. Those bouquets were Stella's vases of normalcy, like the big bunches of chrysanthemums and gladiolas that came with sympathy cards after Daddy died. Now she is gone, I could care less about the property. I pay a kid to come round and mow the lawn once a month, while I sit on the porch and make sure he goes back over the parts he missed. That's good enough.

"Choose whatever you like, Stella, and we'll take it home." The flower shop was overflowing with colour and scent.

Stella wouldn't speak to me but she was good at hand control. Do this. Do that. She had me park her in front of a huge funeral wreath that had a ribbon covered in Chinese characters, and fixated on the florist filling the last holes in the Styrofoam with white lilies and carnations.

She pointed to the grisly wreath.

"No, Stella," I said firmly. I generally handled those situations with tough love – "No, you can't have another drink." "No, you can't have a chocolate bar. " "No, I won't turn up the heat." – and she usually reacted with the rage of a two-year-old, teeth gritted and fists clenched by her sides. "That wreath belongs to a dead person. You are not dead yet." I spun her wheelchair into a bank of glorious orchids. "Choose."

Stella chose a hundred and eighty-seven dollars' worth of calla lilies and white hydrangeas, and I let her. It was her money, after all. She had her pension and the insurance cheques. The florist wrapped her huge bouquet in layers of tissue, tied them with a wide pink ribbon and put them in her lap.

It was a warm summer morning. My mother was quite a sight flying down the street, past lawns filled with sprinkler rainbows and starlings hunting for leatherjackets, in her bib and curlers with an outrageous bunch of expensive blooms in her lap and me running behind, wondering if what was left of her hair would fall. We were both laughing; both of us loving speed, having sex feelings.

I swear she was humming, "Get me to the church on time."

EPHESUS

On the other side of the door, Mahmoud apologized for the stuck door. "It so warm, both sides, door bigger," he said, perspiration beading on his forehead. "Don't worry. I turn off heat."

I admit that in the few minutes he took to rescue us from the steam bath I had visions of cooking alive or having a heart attack or a stroke in the *hamam*.

"Not a bad way to off somebody in Turkey," I said to Güzel, who appeared more embarrassed than worried. "Is this the door to Hell?"

"Other direction," he answered. "Be patient."

While we waited for Mahmoud, he began a parable.

"Am I in it?" I asked, as he began his breathless explanation to the slosh of what I assumed was cold water against the other side of the *hamam* door.

"Yes."

"Go ahead then. We like to watch the movies of our lives when death is imminent."

"Do you remember when we were in the spice market in Istanbul?"

"Yes."

"The spice-seller offered you an aphrodisiac."

"Yes, *lokum*."

"Was he offering romance or candy?"

"Both?" I say, confused. "Either?"

"Good answers."

The door came unstuck and we gathered our things while Mahmoud made a thousand apologies.

"All's well that ends well," I said.

We went back to the hotel and drank *rakı* beside the pool. The night sky was beautiful. "You should be the one writing stories," he said, when I told him once again how frightened I had been in the bath.

"Wasn't a newspaper editor in Ankara recently shot for his views? Wasn't my room searched?"

"Yes. Maybe," he answered. "Still, it sounds like you've been reading too much detective fiction."

"What is it they say about the truth being stranger than fiction?" I asked.

"In Turkey, we don't live our lives worrying about what *might* happen. We improvise with what *has* happened."

"So, I have just had one of my Turkish lessons?"

"That's right." He laughed and his laughter dissipated my lust. I watched it scatter in the heavens.

"What was that?" he asked.

"A falling star."

I think these feelings must have fallen in the pool. There was a splash followed by incandescent ripples. Something electric swooned in the water.

"Do you see it?" I asked. It looked like tinfoil burning in the fireplace.

"Yes, " he said. "That is wet brain."

"Do I understand Turkey now?"

"You're off to a good start." I notice his accent has disappeared.

⚬

Last night, while I lay awake in bed, waiting for god knows what – Güzel or the intruder who smells like orange blossoms – I heard a noise like a mouse tiptoeing through the crack of light under my door. When I got up, I saw that it was a note. I opened the door to see who had brought it, but there was no one in the hall.

The note said, "Ağrı Dağı." That was all.

I assumed it was from Güzel. I know he types because I have heard the soft click of his computer keys over the phone, and, by the way, I hate it when people do that. They think I can't hear, but I do. I think it is rude to type and talk.

⚬

Despite not sleeping last night, I woke up early and drove Güzel to Ephesus in the rented car. He insisted that we get to the ruins before noon, and he was right. At 8 a.m., the heat was already unbearable.

"I got a note last night," I said, as I snapped my seatbelt shut. "Was it from you?"

"Did I sign it?" Güzel asked enigmatically.

"Of course not. If you had, I wouldn't have asked."

"Then it wasn't me. What did it say, if you don't mind my asking?"

"Ağrı Dağı."

"That is Mount Ararat."

"I know. I looked it up on the hotel computer. What do you suppose it means?"

"Perhaps it's a tourist promotion. Greenpeace has built an ark near the mountain to draw attention to climate change."

"Why wouldn't it say so? I subscribe to Greenpeace. They don't send out cryptic bulletins. They give general information and ask for donations."

"It could have been meant for another hotel guest, or did you ask anyone else where you might find snow in the middle of summer?"

"No."

"It does answer your question. If you want to hear the silence of God, Mount Ararat would be the right place. Some scholars say the real Noah's Ark is there. They have seen its skeleton in satellite photos."

Because I don't want to offend Turkishness, I refrain from saying, "What if I went to Mount Ararat and all I heard was the sound of gunfire, Turks shooting Armenians?" But I do think it.

"God is fierce and these are fierce times," he says; and I am not sure if he has read my mind or if he is referring to floods and other disasters or the Arab Spring.

"Ararat is melting like ice cream," I say. "That is why they were able to see the remains of the ark."

"Ararat means Fire Mountain in my language. It is a volcano."

~ॐ~

It is already fifty degrees in the shade and the sun is still low in the sky. Yet, the air-conditioned tour buses disgorge hundreds of intrepid red-faced tourists with water bottles. They are all dressed as if for a safari, in khaki with the hats I've seen advertised in the back pages of the *New Yorker* magazine. In their drabs, they look like wilted salad.

Güzel and I have opted against guides and headsets. We are seeing Ephesus at our own pace.

"My father managed a theatre called the Odeon," I say, standing in front of the small concert hall. I close my eyes and read his luminous sign, ODEON THEATRE.

"This one was built two centuries after the death of Jesus," Güzel tells me, as I recall details from home, the fake Corinthian columns and the slight rake of the seats.

"Can we sit here for a minute?"

The sun is merciless. We finish our water and marvel that neither of us is peeing more than once or twice a day. All the liquid is used up in the cooling of our bodies. What would a pig do in this climate? Do Jews and Muslims abhor them for their lack of sweat glands? Isn't sweating what separates the hunter from his prey, the key to human supremacy?

"This is where we all come together," Güzel explains. "Muslims, Christians, Jews. Mary came here with John after the Romans crucified Jesus. St. Paul argued with the Roman idolaters in this very city. Can you feel the presence?"

"I do." Earlier, I heard a cab driver tell a woman with a child in a wheelchair that the taxi fare to Mary's House, a short distance away, possibly only five hundred metres, was fifty dollars. When I commented on the high price of miracles, Güzel shrugged his shoulders and said, "Taxi drivers have to eat. Americans deserve to pay more."

Beyond the ruins lie the mud flats that bred the mosquitoes that gave the Ephesians malaria and emptied the ancient town. "Do we have to thank the mosquitoes for the preservation of

Ephesus?" I ask. "What would it look like now if people still lived here?" Now would be the time to tell him. The story stops here, or starts. Who would I be without plague and famine? How biblical! But this moment segues into the next. We are seamless.

"Who can say? Once the harbour was silted up, ships would have stopped coming."

"Do you think Mary came by ship?"

"Probably. Apart from the Lydian farmers and merchants travelling overland, most outsiders traveled on boats in those days. Now everyone arrives in airplanes."

"Not the American air force."

"No, can you imagine what would have happened to my country if the Yankees had been given permission to strike at Iraq and probably Iran from bases here? All this antiquity would have been destroyed."

"Wouldn't the Axis of Freedom respect the ruin sites?"

"Did they respect them in Iraq? What about Nagasaki, Dresden and London? What is sacred to people who make war?"

"So that is why the taxi drivers charge fifty dollars to go to Mary's House. They are putting a value on miracles."

"The Muslims revere Mary too. She is mentioned in the Qur'an."

"I'll bet the hyper-Christian American right doesn't know that."

"They don't know anything."

"I hope they don't think I am an American," I say. "Someone is watching me."

"Someone is watching *over* you, Madeleine," Güzel laughs.

"So you know all about Jazz?"

"Of course I do. Jazz is my favourite."

"Do you want to hear Sweet Papa Lowdown play in Izmir this evening?"

"Of course I do. You know jazz is female, improvisation being the mother of evolution."

"Let's keep moving, keep on keepin' on," he says. "We can't sit still for long. It is too hot."

Tourists or flocks of goats inhabit every shadow here. The tourists move from shade to shade with their guidebooks while the goats stand their ground, chewing the leaves from low-hanging branches.

At the Library of Celcus with its roof open to the sky, Güzel tells me there is a tunnel leading to the brothel on the other side of the marble street. "The men of Ephesus told their women they were going to the library; and then they disappeared under the ground."

I think he expects me to be indignant on behalf of the wives. He looks surprised when I say, "I hope they were prepared to answer questions about the tablets they were reading." I am familiar with lies and ruses. The proximity of mind and body pleases me. The library and brothel define the parameters of my life.

PAPER HORSES

My mother loved hot summer days and nights and her Keely Smith and Louis Prima recording of "Fever." She'd get all dolled up in a sexy dress and high heels and lip-sync with the abused diva. She told me it drove my father crazy when she did that. By then, Louis Prima and Keeley Smith had broken up and the whole world knew he beat the stuffing out of her because she was more popular than he was, but that didn't stop my mother from worshipping the singer. Sometimes, when she wasn't playing Fred and Ginger, she called my poor dead dad "Louis." "Me and Louis," she would start saying and I would cover my ears and close my eyes. I saw fire licking my closed lids. The room was on fire. The house was on fire. Our yard was on fire. The whole damn neighbourhood was burning. The only good thing was the neighbourhood dogs howling in harmony with fire engines. Dogs are smart, at least when it comes to pitch.

Don't get me wrong. I liked fire, but I disrespected firewater and all who sailed on her, especially my mother.

I don't know if Coon discovered fire on his own, but he might have. Who would have shown a wild boy who had lost his mother in a crosswalk how to make sparks? Maybe he stole matches, but I never saw any. Coon's fire was the only light in his boy cave, with its shelves filled with cans and jars, found table and chairs, and his bed made in a rock shelf with cedar boughs and blankets he ripped off clotheslines. He never let the embers go out, even in summer.

My dad used to say he had a fire in his belly. Coon's fire was real, a pile of ash and live embers surrounded by rocks. There was lots of dead wood in the bushes around the cave, and I proved my usefulness by gathering and stacking broken branches in neat piles where we wouldn't trip over them.

I'd learned a thing or two in my life on earth and I shared them with Coon. Before he went to spirit, my father showed me how to make saltpetre horse races by drawing lines with a solution of potassium nitrate on cardboard and lighting the tracks. He made me promise not to tell Stella. She would have busted a gut. We did it behind the garage because she hardly ever left the kitchen, except to go dancing, when he was alive.

It wasn't hard getting the saltpetre. I went to the drugstore on Tillicum Road and explained I needed it for my horse. I looked like the kind of girl that might have been horse crazy. I would have if I had a real family. I'd spent a couple of summers hanging around the barns mucking out stalls and cleaning tack, waiting for rich kids saddled with unwanted ponies to let me ride them. The thing about rich kids is they haven't the foggiest clue about sharing. To them, horses are just another inconvenience, like too many pairs of shoes. They don't need them, but they resist sharing.

Coon had his paper horses and I had mine. We gave them outrageous names like The Drunk Mother from Hell and The Avenging Angel of Traffic Fatalities and watched them burn up the track. Whoever lost had to do dares. I showed Coon my tits and he ate red ants – that kind of thing. Coon did everything I asked him to do and I kept up as best I could on the dangerous dares, even though I was fatter than him and not as good at rambling.

We called our life in the woods "rambling." I got to know every rock and tree and we must have marked most of them one time or another. The night rambles made me nervous and I pissed like a nervous puppy, leaving a trail of puddles behind me. If my mother had been a bloodhound and interested in my whereabouts in the middle of the night, when most kids were sound asleep in their beds, I would have been as easy to find in the forest as Hansel and Gretel's pussy-whipped dad.

In a sense, I had to find myself. Short of turning myself into a human flare like those Buddhist nuns who doused themselves with gasoline during the Vietnam War, I could see no better way to light my way than setting off fireworks. Perhaps Stella, my imploded star, might even hear me explode across the firmament. At the very least, I could identify my own shadow on the wall where my wild friend made his home.

I raided my father's basement workshop. I stole SOS pads from under the kitchen sink. They made a wonderful blue light in the fire. I grazed for over-the-counter items in various stores, one thing here, and one thing there, so the dots wouldn't be connected should I be apprehended for taking a five-finger discount. I made hydrogen balloons and watched them explode like the *Hindenburg* on that tragic day in New York. I lit bags of Cheesies on fire. They are pure petroleum. Boom!

At night, I wrote my mother's name in the salt water in the Gorge, so some sentient being might read it – Earth calling Stella. Hello?

"Where have you been?" I heard her ask in the grey light cast from the electric eye beaming test patterns in our living room.

"Out."

"Out?" She made the whole word, including the "t", so there was the possibility she might have been sober.

"Yeah, out, walking, thinking, out."

"You shouldn't be Oh You Tee alone at night."

"I was with my friend."

"Your im-a-gin-ary friend?" She drew the word out.

"I told you, Stella; he's real and his home is real."

"And ours isn't, Little Miss Critical?"

"How come you never call me by my name? I have a name, you know. I'll bet you've forgotten it."

"I am not going to dignify that with an answer." My own dignity swooshed down the toilet. I was blubbering, just like she had the last time we'd argued about Coon. Snot bubbled out of my nose. The only thing I could do was go to my room and slam the door hard.

When I woke up the next morning, my room smelled different. The whole house smelled different. The radio was on. The TV was off. My mother was in the kitchen and she was actually making breakfast.

"Both sides or sunny side up?" she asked, holding the egg turner in one hand and a cigarette in the other.

"Whatever." I slumped into a kitchen chair. Was I dreaming?

"Got any plans for today," she asked, as if the question were as worn as an old piece of flannel.

"Yeah, rambling."

"Into the woods, eh," she said cheerfully. "I think I'll have a nap. You kept me awake last night, young lady."

I was in shock. Stella had risen from her Easyboy recliner like a ghost from the garbage-strewn muck in the Gorge estuary. If her resurrection was real and I wasn't imagining it, then the new situation would take some getting used to.

"Sorry, Mum." I tried the word and looked away, in case it spat back at me like mud from a passing bicycle.

She made me an egg in the hole. It's almost impossible to ruin egg in the hole, but she did manage to break the yolk. I put it on a paper plate and left, closing the screen door gently, just in case she was real, and fed my breakfast to Frend as soon as I got past the garage. I had to tell Coon what had happened. Sometimes, good news is as hard to understand as bad. It helps to play it by someone else. You hear yourself talking. The bad ideas kind of surface like stones in the garden and you can toss them aside or make a wall out of them.

I talked my head off all day. When I got hungry, I opened a can of pork and beans we'd piked from the Safeway and we ate them cold. I like them that way. Maybe, I thought, Stella was a grown-up version of Snow White. She got poisoned by grief and had to sleep it off. Maybe it was time for her to wake up and be a mother. It was not quite too late. That was what I wanted, wasn't it? That was why I walked like an elephant when she was sleeping and why I lit my signal fires. Maybe she heard one of my hydrogen balloons popping or saw her name reflected in the firmament when I wrote it in salt water.

When I finished talking, I was exhausted. I lay down on Coon's little bed of cedar boughs and fell asleep smelling the wood and listening to the sparks from his fire. When I woke up, it was night and Coon was gone foraging. I felt fresh and new. Maybe my mother had put a candle in the window for me, like her Irish relatives who lit beacons for strangers and missing family. We both missed my dad. He had betrayed her by dying so young and so suddenly. It wasn't fair to either of us. We both deserved to be babies again. Now it was my turn. Stella would morph back into Mum and take care of me. I deserved it. I felt as light as a fat girl can hurtling lickety-split down the hill toward home. I was ready. Stella was ready. We could start again.

The porch light was on. The television was off. Stella was waiting for me in her Easyboy, a half-finished tray of drinks beside her. "Er 'ate," she said. Stella had misplaced her consonants once again.

I landed hard. The voice that came out of the dark living room was as thick as a brick wall. "I'm not gonna tell you 'gain. There's no fren'," she slurred. "I saw you talkin' to yourself. You made 'im up. You're jus' a big fat load of tweedy, Mudder."

"I am not your mother," I screamed. "I am not your fucking mother and you are nobody."

"Don't tell me 'bout nobody. You wrote that book."

"I hate you," I said under my breath, because I was deciding at that very moment to burn our house down.

Well, not exactly the house, although it did cross my mind to decorate the living room with the Christmas lights abandoned in the basement when my father died, and set fire to Stella's blanket while she lay passed out in her Easyboy. That would have been something. The grey-blue light from the television, the Christmas lights, the burning chair. Her blanket already looked like Swiss cheese, there were so many cigarette burns in it. It would have been no stretch of the imagination to accept that Stella had fallen asleep once too often with a live cigarette in her hand.

But I didn't do that. I loved my mother. I didn't want her to die a horrible death. I wanted her to wake up from her terrible sleep and actually see me. I had made myself fat, noisy and whiney, an unavoidable obnoxious presence, but she still didn't get it.

In India, they burn widows on their husbands' funeral pyres. Otherwise, the poor women get their heads shaved and are abandoned by their families to beg in white saris. My mother, Stella, Dad's little sun, had chosen to burn slowly. It was my duty to show her what she had done.

I made a hell of a pile on the front lawn. It took me from dawn until late morning, but Stella didn't notice because she was sleeping the sleep of the damned. I dragged her mattress down the stairs and covered it with chairs, tables and books, anything that would burn. I covered the furniture with her pretty dresses. She didn't need them any more. They were for him. Everything was for him. I collected his clothes. I took my two favourite girl dolls, Stella and Mother, wrapped them in shawls with sparkly threads and laid them on top of my dad's desk, which I had covered with Stella's muskrat coat. Then I poured gasoline over the whole works and went in the house to wake her up.

I slammed the front door. "Wake up, Stella," I yelled, then went closer and bellowed in her ear. She reeked of sweat, smoke, booze, and vomit, the bilious kind that you burp up and swallow. I took her to the window.

"Wait here," I said.

"Why? The sun's in my eyes." She blinked.

"Because when you look, you will see yourself."

I ran out of the house and dropped a match into a waste-basket filled with old family photographs. I dumped its contents on the pile, which ignited with a terrible sound. "How much noise would it take to raise hell? I was about to find out that real hell was silent."

"Wake up!" I screamed. "Wake up, Stella. Wake up, neighbourhood. The child city is burning. The child is burning. Anyone gonna save her?"

I ran back in the house. "Your house is on fire. Your child is burning. Are you just going to stand there? Do something, Stella."

For once.

My mother thought if she stopped when my father died, then she could keep it all – the memories, the smell of his shoes in the closet, his half-finished bottles of whiskey. He would recognize the house, his wife and child, his dog, his flowers. He would know when he passed over our house on his angel drive-by that nothing had changed. She thought she could sedate herself with whiskey and me with despair, but she hadn't counted on me. Sooner or later, I was going to do something. It was death, and we were living. To live like that was an abomination.

If she was a star stuck in my father's heaven, then I was his volatile ride. I would rather fling myself into the firmament than wait helpless on the sharp edge of the world. I grabbed her hair and pushed her face into the window. "Look!"

A fire engine came and put out the fire I had started. The fire chief came and gave me a lecture. Stella stopped speaking to me. Forever.

SHOOTING STARS

There is no one else sitting beside the moonlit pool. The hotel guests must be asleep in their air-conditioned rooms, or out promenading on the seawall alongside local families whose children are restless because of the heat. I have never seen so many kids up so late, eating the strange Turkish ice cream that tastes like marshmallow and sticks so well to the scoops that the ice cream vendors clown with it, turning the cones upside down and pretending to drop them. I wonder if the children dangling on balconies are also sticky. Is that why their mothers are nowhere in sight? They must trust gravity. Did my mother trust gravity? I doubt she gave it a thought.

If I'd had kids, they would have had strict bedtimes, even during heat waves. I don't know why some parents can't understand how important it is for children to have predictable lives – shelter and schedules, bedtimes and meals on time. I hated growing up without rules and schedules.

Once again, Güzel and I are lying on parallel sun cots, dipping watermelon in cloudy glasses of *rakı* and watching the night sky. I have trouble believing that I am the same person who, half a world and half a lifetime away, stole out of my house to lie beside an alleged imaginary boy under the same stars.

"Did you see that?" Güzel asks. It is his turn. This is our call and response.

"What was it?"

"A shooting star."

"Did you make a wish?"

"Of course."

We compare mythologies. How could they be so different and yet so similar? If I had seen the falling star, I would have wished that Güzel would gather me up in his arms and carry me past the concierge in the lobby up the winding stairs to my room. Why would I wish that, I think just as quickly? What would be the point? He would lie on my bed and wait for me to make love to him. Then he would politely, but firmly, ask me not to kiss him on the mouth. I know that is the invisible line between women like me and the women men like Güzel fall in love with and marry. I would pleasure him anyway. Perhaps I would wash his groin with grief and he would say he was sorry, kiss my eyes and swallow my tears. He would leave my room before morning. He might even leave the hotel, but not before buying me a bus ticket to Kars.

"I had a friend once. We slept under the stars every night and we wished and wished."

"Did you get your wishes, Madeleine?"

"No. He thought his mother had been cut up and made into stars and I thought my father was up there with her. We wanted to rapture up to them, but we always woke up on earth, just as we were."

"But you were already lucky to have one another. Perhaps that was enough good luck."

"My mother kept insisting the boy wasn't real, and then he disappeared."

"Was she right?"

"No." What is real, anyway? Isn't desire real?

"Then perhaps he had gone to find his mother."

"Tell me if you see him."

"I think I do." Güzel points. "Can you see the boy with the net? He is trying to capture every star in the heavens."

"You are a beautiful man, Güzel."

Perhaps he will still be here in the morning.

ONE LAST THING

My mother was a mess from the moment my father died until a few minutes before she died. "Slattern" would be the right word. She aged twenty years in the time it takes to say, "widow." I watched her shut down and I heard her shut up. After the fire, she communicated by writing notes. All I got from her were grocery lists; always the same, so why did she bother?

Tonic water

Lemons

Chip steaks

Cigarettes

Matches

Bread

Mustard

Toilet paper

The rest I had to think of myself. This went on and on until one day she just made loopy lines. After six years in her rest home, on the day the Twin Towers fell in New York, she quit eating and drinking and turned herself into Sleeping Beauty.

I've seen this kind of transformation a number of times now and so I know I didn't imagine it. When my mother pulled up her covers and closed her eyes for the last time, I was sure she could see my dad standing on the horizon holding an armful of lilies, a big tangerine sky behind him; the same sun that does its lyrical descent over Sultanahmet setting on both of them.

Like an infant pushing its way through the birth canal, she was rushing to meet him. My mum was a baby with a deadline, puffing and pushing, giving birth to herself.

In those moments, her skin became soft and smooth, her hair opened like the petals around a flower. Her hands folded themselves exquisitely on her chest. She breathed; and the sound of her breathing was passionate.

"Get out of my way," she said. "You slut." Those were her last words, and they were not spoken to me.

The word for slut in Turkish is *orispu*. I love it. *Oris* for mouth and *pu*, well, that's shit. Shitspeaker. Yes.

Stella left a letter she had written when I was still a child. It was in her underwear drawer, hidden by a bag of lavender. On the outside she had written the word "Mother," but inside she started off with "Madeleine." She wrote: "Dear Madeleine, I know I am a bad mother. When I look into your eyes I see judgment. Can I hope for some understanding? Would you forgive me if I could find the way to love you more? I want to. I need your father to show me, but how can I make a dead man love me enough? When I looked at his body, I wanted to shake him alive so I could ask him. It wasn't me who killed him. It was her. He had his first heart attack at home, but the second one happened in the hospital. When I rushed in to say goodbye, she was still in his room, her hair a mess and lipstick and tears all over her face, and she had the nerve to pretend she was just visiting. I knew. All those nights and weekends he was supposed to be working, she was working her candy counter. What a fool I was to order a couch for his office so he could take naps."

Didn't my mother know he was riding the angel of death? My mother was as thick as cardboard. After I read her letter, I got every one of her precious Daddy-given china teacups out of the glass vitrine and smashed them.

MUSTAFA LAUGHS

The former dervish lives on top of a mountain near Kas. Güzel is navigating. He appears to know the road, a steep and winding nightmare with a sheer cliff and no guardrails. My foot is nervous on the gas pedal. We are driving at night, the headlights sweeping rock as we take the hairpin curves. I am terrified but Güzel reminds me, when I dig my fingernails into the steering wheel, that many Turks live on mountains and move as carefully as goats to avoid falling rocks.

"Talk to me," he says. "It will help free your mind."

"I am not supposed to end up here," I say. "I was going to Kars, not Kas. I misheard what the band members told me on the plane. They were heading to Kas, nowhere near the silence of snow, where Noah parked his boat and Russian spirit wrestlers made an attempt to farm in peace and—"

"What does it matter?" Güzel interrupts. "One letter. That is nothing."

"It's because of the book."

"Kars means 'snow' in Turkish, but you can have snow anywhere you want."

"You mean anywhere that starts with the letter K, like *kuku*?

"Why not," he laughs? "At least you are going to a higher altitude. That is close."

"It is also closer to the sun."

When we arrive at the summit, his friend Mustafa comes out of his stone cottage with a large bowl of rice with fragrant herbs and chunks of lamb and, after inviting us to wash our hands in a small fountain built into the outside wall, leads us to a platform built over a sheer cliff. We settle into the big cushions in his aerie and eat from the communal bowl, dipping in flatbread. The food tastes like pieces of the moon. "Don't look down," Güzel jokes. "Look up." The stars are even more intense than they were in Cesme.

"There is nothing between us and God on this mountain," says Mustafa, who looks more like a hybrid surfer hippie than a monk with his long hair and torn shorts.

"Is that why you are here?" I ask, as I try to imagine him wearing a long skirt and tombstone hat like the dervishes I saw whirling in Istanbul.

"Yes. You understand." When Mustafa smiles, I see in the shimmering light that he is missing teeth. Sound whistles through the black holes in his smile. "I spin and pray and still I am depressed with world, so I come here out of world and make poetry and music."

While Güzel explains that musicians and writers come to Mustafa's mountain for sacred experiences, our host runs back to the house to get his *saz*. I look down and realize that the plank bridge to the platform crosses a deep chasm.

"What if he falls?" I ask Güzel – a stupid question. I think Mustafa has prayed his way out of a hole deeper than the slice in the side of the mountain on which this frail structure perches.

In the peace of this night, I understand what is being offered. There are no thought police here, like the ones reading my mind on the streets or trespassing in my hotel rooms. I am afraid of the *Jandarma* with their automatic rifles, and the stories of captivity and torture I have read in the world press. So long as I am afraid, I will learn nothing. Mustafa knows better.

I think Güzel is similarly enlightened. That may be the reason why he is with me. He may be my spirit guide, or am I deluding myself? Is it wrong thinking to assume that wisdom comes from men? Am I copping to the biological behaviour of women who lust after wise men in order to recreate wisdom? How long will we believe that we are as strong, as intelligent, and as talented as the elixir we sip? Is this the purgatory of girls whose fathers die young or is it an inherent gender fault?

"My *saz* is *bozuk*," Mustafa laughs. There are, he points out, cracks in the wood, but he believes it sounds better that way.

"We are all *bozuk*," I say, "in our various ways. We have a poet in our country. He wrote, 'Forget your perfect offerings/ There is a crack in everything/That's how the light gets in.'"

"We know this man in Turkey. He is Leonard Cohen," Mustafa says.

"A Jew," I say.

"A Buddhist." Mustafa adds.

I feel as though I might have arrived at my moment. The night is balmy, the heat moderated by a wind that rises off the Mediterranean and climbs the side of the mountain. Our bellies are filled with comforting hospitality. Even the stars are warm.

"Is this why you came to Turkey?" Güzel asks, while Mustafa tunes his instrument.

"I told you I came to hear God and help Iman, but now I am distracted. I can't even read a map." I laugh. "Not that there are any maps in Turkey."

"We have stars for map. We have mountain and minaret. God listen. We don't need map for God. I will try to call him for you," Mustafa says gently. "In old day before Rumi, music not allowed in worship. Now, for seven hundred years, we have art, dance, music."

Seven hundred years ago, I think, our Aboriginal people were circling the fire and dancing. We were about to come and put out the fire, or die trying. I shiver and, even though he is lying on a cushion several feet away from me, I think I feel Güzel's arm cover my shoulders like a soft snowfall, but it is Mustafa's blanket.

"In my culture, many men refuse to dance."

"In your culture, they might see dancing as sexual, not social," Güzel says without embarrassment.

"When I was a little girl, I would spin and spin until I felt so dizzy I fell down."

"What did you see then?" Güzel asks.

"I saw stars."

"Exactly," Mustafa says.

"Now you hear God in the air between stars." Güzel makes a big gesture that includes the whole sky.

"Or the holes in snowflakes," I answer.

"Yes," Güzel agrees, "windows like dragon breath."

As Mustafa begins to play sacred notes on his instrument, I hear it. Silence does not exist by itself. Of course, it was there all along, but I was blind, or deaf. I must make my own snow.

"Maybe Pamuk means that snow exists in our heads. Kars could be Brigadoon or the Emerald City. It wouldn't matter. We are always rushing to get somewhere before it melts, the point being that we are already there."

"Now you think like Turk," Mustafa says.

One night before I left home, I went to the outdoor theatre in Beacon Hill Park and watched the old Beatles movie, *Yellow Submarine*. While the band danced on a field of polka dots, Ringo picked one up and put it in his pocket. "I've got an 'ole in me pocket," he said.

I've got a hole in me pocket and the pain is slowly leaking out, filling the valley below us with beautiful music.

ALMOST MIDNIGHT

Tonight, Sweet Papa Lowdown is playing on a platform stage set up on a rocky beach near Kas. The concert started late because of the heat. It is almost midnight and they are still in the first set. I am sitting alone at the band table, with a few *mezze* plates in front of me. Like a mountain goat, I graze the olives, fava beans and *boregi*. I like this careful separation of food.

The band girls are sitting together: the mandolinist's wife, the two beautiful sisters and Françoise, their father's French lover. Güzel is off somewhere writing. I rode the *dolmuş* minibus to the outdoor club. Did I know, Naomi asked me earlier, that *dolmuş* comes from the same root as the *mezze* wrapped in grape leaves? No, I did not, but I like the idea of travellers wrapped in the safety of leaves from ancient vines and a minibus that departs when it is full.

The chairs sit lopsided in gravel. I want to dance, but I am worried about spraining my ankle in my impractical sandals. A handful of English girls have come in a hotel shuttle bus. They peep like a flock of birds and the chirping gets louder the more they drink.

The English girls are not afraid to dance on gravel in their platform shoes tied with ribbons. Their feet hardly touch the pebbles as they dance alone and in a flock, joining and separating. The girls are young and I enjoy watching them. Jeff is singing "When the Sun Goes Down in Harlem." One girl spins like a dervish, saying over and over, "Foster, foster." She spins perilously close to Doug, who is holding on to his sax for dear life and does not look amused. I assume she means "faster." I am not sure whether she is giving orders to herself, to the band, or to life itself.

Everything stops. It is the end of the song, but she keeps on spinning until her skirt lifts over her hips and her friends rescue her. The English girl is not wearing underpants.

The band segues from embarrassment into a slow *taksim* introduction and Rick begins to sing "Istanbul." "Foster," the English girl shouts again and her friends abandon her, making their way to my table, inviting me to dance with them.

"You shouldn't be alone."

"No," I say, and they insist, taking my hands and pulling me into the rocky space between the beach chairs and the band. They dance in a slow circle, holding hands, throwing their heads back and moving their hips. My feet forget to be nervous. I find my hips. Something else takes over. It isn't the notes or the words – it's the sound of the world turning.

Sitting down for a glass of *rakı* during the band break, I ask Rick to tell me what he loves most about playing the blues in Turkey.

"I love it when I catch a totally enshrouded woman tapping her foot to the music. Just when I don't expect a reaction, there it is. It has nothing to do with listening. That is conscious. It happens when we feel it together."

Yes, we do, when we allow ourselves to be moved. I have learned something special tonight. We are all here: Iman, my mother, the Pinks (Sweet Papa's girls), these hormonal English hounds off their leashes, when we feel the deeper music.

GONE FOR GOOD

I never liked the colour red. Red hits me with a closed fist, right in the guts. *Pouf.* It takes my wind, or it winds me up so I can't think straight. I wouldn't own a red car, a red dress, or a red pair of shoes. Firm red tomatoes give me the heaves. I threw up all over my breakfast the morning I discovered blood in my soft-boiled egg. Stella said the red spot was a baby chicken, but I could see it was blood, plain and simple.

It was my father who got our first laying hens, and me who looked after them. They pecked the hell out of the garden, which eventually came to resemble a moonscape, and got him a citation for keeping poultry within the city limits. Our Pentecostal neighbours complained about the rooster racket and barnyard sex. Sex to chickens is just a squirt – no flowers, no foreplay, and no words of love. I have no idea why the miraculously born again objected to that. In the end, we shut them up with free eggs. The Pentecostals eventually left, but the eggs are grandfathered in and I still tithe a dozen a week to the new neighbours when my hens are laying.

My father was a rooster, and it can't be said that he lacked romance, even if he did spread it a bit thin. He gave my distraught mother a ruby ring the day after she thought she flushed a baby down the toilet at the age of forty-five. "It was my last chance."

Diamonds surrounded the ruby. "Your heart is protected by sleeping dinosaurs," he told her. I didn't understand at the time, nor did my mother. She cried and cried, but she never took the ring off. He gave me a cigar ring and it tore right away.

One night, when he had been drinking, he confided to me that he had found the ruby ring under a seat in the movie theatre. I wonder why he didn't give it to his candy lady.

My father kept on smoking cigars. I stopped flushing the toilet. How would I know there wasn't a baby in it? Soon after that, my father left us, not in an anonymous swoosh of unconsecrated water circling the drain but in a convoy of wailing sirens. All the dogs in our neighbourhood sang the night my father left our house and didn't come back.

The life insurance wasn't quite enough to live on. I got over my aversion to eggs. We ate a lot of them: fried eggs, chip steaks and eggs, scrambled eggs, egg in the hole – you name it. We called eggs "widow food." When my mother died thirty years and approximately twenty-four thousand eggs and chip steaks and at least a thousand bottles of gin later, the ring slipped off her finger without a struggle. I put it on my pinkie. "My heart is protected by sleeping dinosaurs," I thought whenever I looked at it.

While I was feeding my hens the day of the tsunami that swallowed most of the beaches in Asia, my mother's ring slipped off my fingers and fell into the snow and mud in the chicken yard. There was no such thing as dinosaurs, and God and my father are dead, I keep telling myself, but in my heart of hearts I hoped that one day I would crack open my breakfast egg and find her ruby.

I've never had a passion like the one my mother had for my father. Sometimes I wonder if her loyalty was simple obsession or perversity because she always knew, deep down, that she couldn't have one hundred percent of him. When we were kids, we avoided the pavement cracks. *Step on a crack/break your mother's back.* That was the cardinal sin. Thou shalt not snap thy mother in half the way thy father killed crabs before throwing them in hot water or made her cry out in the night.

I looked for the cracks in my parents' marriage, the broken mirror or smashed concrete that had brought bad luck down on us – but there was nothing to be seen, not even the little touch me game he played with me. To be seen, the phrase that cops use to prosecute motorists who bump into invisible things, is in fact "there to be seen."

Who killed the baby? I never saw it, just took my mother's word that it existed at all. Her terrible weeping was proof of her unrequited love; and her ruby mourning-ring was proof of my father's love for her. Her, her, her; I was so glad to meet Coon and accept another pronoun into my life. Coon was father, brother and friend. He was my map of the wilderness on both sides of our garden fence. Him.

I am a bloodhound when it comes to following my nose. My father used to call me Ole Yeller, because of the haystack colour of my hair and my hounding instincts. "Where is the chocolate?" he'd ask, and make me sniff out an Oh Henry or a Mars bar he'd brought home from work. My father smelled of cigars and hair tonic. My mother smelled of gin and cigarettes. My dog smelled wet.

Coon slept in a bed made of cedar branches and cooked over an open fire. I can't remember his face or the sound of his voice after all these years, but I will never forget his smell. His brackish odours had the stink of innocence. Unlike most kids, I was evolving backwards to a time I barely recalled. By the time Coon came to steal fruit from our garden, I was pretty hard-bitten. There wasn't much romance in living with the burnt-out star that had fallen from the ceiling of my father's movie theatre. Coon was my chance to grab a piece of child-hood before it all went up in her cigarette smoke.

We were kids, side by each, both of us orphans. My mother said I made him up. Maybe so. My father promised an angel would visit me. What would it have mattered if he were material or immaterial? He was real to me. His cave was real. She saw that for herself. "You did it!" she said, in the firm belief that a splash of reality would bring me to my senses and keep my hand on her plow. Someone had to wash her widow's weeds, and I had to keep going to school or sooner or later she'd have the authorities on her back.

I did it, all right. I started the fire that silenced her and dis-appeared him. I was on my own from that moment to this.

I was sure the moment I met Blackflies Littlebear that I had met him before. Blackflies' carving shed was a storage locker a few doors down from my massage studio. One sunny day, while I was taking a break, eating an egg sandwich out in the parking lot, he blocked my sun. He smelled like trees. For a minute I thought he was Coon coming back.

"How much does it cost to get a massage?" he asked.

I told him.

"Do you trade?"

"What for?"

"Carving."

"Maybe. I'd have to see what you've got."

I'd already sniffed Blackflies' woodsy locker and wondered who and what was inside it. He was all set up with his tools hanging on the wall the way my father had arranged his – with the outlines drawn on the drywall in felt pen, so he'd always know where they were. I breathed in and felt myself getting bent out of shape. Blackflies Littlebear had a neat wall of tools, long black hair, and he smelled of cedar. What more could a girl ask for? That was ten years ago.

Another wall was hung with masks in various stages of completion.

"This here's *Wild Woman*," he said, taking down a round face with real hair. "I'm making her for my sister."

He told me the stories of eagle, bear and mosquito, trying on each mask and showing me a dance or a bit of a song. When Blackflies let me wear his masks, I felt free to look at his body. He wore jeans, a Wounded Knee T-shirt and sneakers. I could see the shapes of his muscles through the tight cloth. When he turned to the wall, I fell in love with his neat little bum.

I traded Blackflies a beautiful hummingbird mask inlaid with abalone for six massages. He said I'd made a good choice.

"You were eating when I met you," he said, "just like a hummingbird. I never met anyone that liked food so much." I didn't tell him that I used to be fat, that a miracle had melted it all away, everything but the breasts.

The first time, I gave Blackflies a back and shoulder rub. He'd complained that his shoulders got sore from doing his work. Part of the problem was his posture. He sat on a stool to carve with the wood in his lap. I had a client who was a ukulele player and he had the same problem. I told them both they had to sit up straight for their backs, but neither of them listened. Blackflies Littlebear wasn't going to learn anything from me. He was himself and that wasn't going to change.

My carver was shy about undressing in front of me, so I massaged him fully dressed. I've seen Indians swimming with their clothes on and I thought it was because they couldn't afford bathing suits. He told me the missionaries had made his people shy.

"They fucked our ancestors," he said, his face going dark. "That made us ashamed forever."

"What about you, Blackflies? Who fucked you?"

"Sister Teresa."

"Your sister?"

"No, a nun. I went to Residential School. I broke some rules and I got punished."

"Like what?"

"I spoke our language to my brothers and sisters and I wet my bed, so I had to clean her office, and, when I was done, she did bad things to me."

"Like what?"

"I had to take off all my clothes and she beat me with a ruler until I bled. Then she made me beat her."

"I wouldn't hurt you like that."

The next time, Blackflies took his jeans off and I massaged his legs and his ass, but I was careful to tell him the muscles were connected. I didn't want to scare him away because he was the best-looking man I had ever seen, with or without clothes. His skin was smooth and muscular, lovely to touch.

When I let my hand creep up his thigh, he made little happy noises like a puppy licking his bowl.

I wonder if it is possible to forget pain. Is that why we fall in love?

When I touched Blackflies, I closed my eyes and smelled carbon dioxide. I saw Coon standing naked in the summer rain, laughing and telling me the rain was his shower from heaven.

"How did you get your name?" I asked him one day.

"There are too many flies in the North. You've got to stay ahead of them. I was a restless baby, so they called me 'Blackflies.'"

"Do you think they gave you a good name?"

"I never stopped moving."

"Would you like to take my dad's old car for a spin?"

Blackflies said he knew how to drive a car with a gearshift, so we pulled the blackberry vines off the garage door. The Chev was covered in dust, but it started right up.

"My dad parked it here the day he had his heart attack. That was twenty years ago, and no one's driven it since."

He backed out of the driveway. "Where to?"

"Just take me somewhere fast." I wanted to speed and be afraid of speed. I'd had that feeling before and it was good. Mr. Gudewill called it sex feelings, what happens to a cat if you scratch the base of its tail.

"Faster," I said, when he got out on the Pat Bay Highway.

"Just this once," he said. "Once is enough."

Blackflies was telling me something, but I was enjoying the stories so much I didn't let myself think about the time when he'd be gone. I even stopped giving extras to my other customers. That meant emptier pockets, but I didn't care.

One night, I dreamed Blackflies had given me a handful of magic mushrooms after his massage. I don't usually remember my dreams because I am such a deep sleeper, but this time I did. "These here are sacred," he said, and I ate them. Before long, the world was beautiful. My bottles sparkled with fairy dust.

"Let's catch a stroll," he said, taking my hand. I felt as if I was walking on the moon. We headed for the woods. I was weightless and the night air embraced me, lifting me up so my feet hardly touched the grass. The colours were beautiful, blues and greens running together in the darkness, stars lighting our way.

"Let's lie down," I said. I thought Blackflies might touch me, but he didn't. We just lay on our backs looking at the galaxies, rising among them, floating free.

"I see God," I said, or was it my dad?

Blackflies heard it first, the voice of an angel.

"Hear that?" he whispered.

"It sounds like a baby," I answered.

"It's right here," he said.

We followed the sounds further into the bush. In a clearing lit by moonlight, a small elf sat talking to himself in the elf language, or *wawa*, as Blackflies often said.

"Who sent him?" I asked.

Blackflies scooped up the elf and we carried him to my house. By the time we got home, he was asleep. The little guy had scabs on his hands and feet.

In the morning, Blackflies wasn't lying beside me as I had hoped in that moment before consciousness when I realized I must have been dreaming.

That day, I asked Blackflies if he'd like to stay at my place.

"No flies on me," he grinned. "I gotta move on," was all he said.

"Why?"

"Because I've finished my work here."

"But you're not finished with me."

"You are my work, " he said.

"I don't get it."

"You will."

The following evening, I turned on the light in my locker and saw a yellow cedar box with a carving of *Dzunu_kwa*, Wild Woman of the Woods, sitting on my massage table. I backed out of the room as if that box had bubonic plague in it. There was no answer when I knocked on Blackflies' door. I tried the latch. It was unlocked, so I went in. The place was empty. Everything was gone: his stool, the tools, the stack of wood, the cans of paint, and the masks and rattles he'd been working on. He'd even scrubbed his "carving shed." It smelled of Pine Sol.

I got it. Blackflies must have driven off in my dad's old Chevrolet and left me the box. His name was carved underneath. I wondered how long he'd been working on it.

For a long time, I would open it up and smell Blackflies Littlebear. That helped me remember what it was like to be with him, and long before that, my summer with Coon, lying on a bed of cedar boughs and frying eggs over his fire.

"Those are rubies," I said about the spots on the eggs, but I knew they were blood.

That made me think about Jesus on the cross and nuns who fall in love with his suffering.

So that was it.

My box has vanished but I still remember the smell of the yellow cedar. I googled his name and found out that Blackflies

Littlebear had died in a car accident three years before I met him.

‹§›

Something goes bump in the night. It could be a dove stuck in the warm tar on the roof above my head. It could be a truck loading up garbage from the hotel, or a drunk, loaded with *raki*, in the hallway, trying to fit his key in the lock and losing his balance. I hear a sound and it wakes me out of a sleep in which someone is gently making love to me, as if a piece of cool silk were being teased down the length of my body. I am annoyed because I don't want the dream to end.

"Who is it?" I whisper. "I know you're there. I can smell you."

There is no answer. While I lie awake, listening, I hear thunder in the distance and then closer. There are flashes of lightning so bright my room lights up as if someone is turning the electric light on and off.

I close my eyes and open them. My mother is standing in the room, wearing the dress she wore the night my father died. "Star!" she says once, and then vanishes.

ROSE-COLOURED GLASSES

Sevmek's letter to the motherboard

Mad is going to the mountain and I believe our time with her is almost over. It remains to be seen what she will hear. Revelation is relative. She might see blood in the snow. Güzel may reveal himself. That option is always open to him.

I'm surprised she didn't mention that her chickens pecked at one another. If she didn't notice then perhaps she wasn't ready to fully understand human nature. That may still be coming to her.

There is an axiom about bullies. They seek victims, just as hens peck at other hens that are already wounded. At about the time Mad's mother lost her ring, a distressed farmer in Petaluma, California, egg basket of the world, whose hens were murdering one another, lifted a sleeve of red eye on his front porch and saw a crimson world through the bottom of his near empty glass. Eureka, he'd made the discovery that, if all that chickens saw was red they would not discern the red spots on one another's white feathers, and the brutal pecking would stop.

The chicken farmer called an optician and had red lenses made for all his flock. No sooner were they fitted with rose-coloured lenses than the cannibalism stopped.

I am surprised it didn't occur to anyone that we could order rose-coloured glasses for the entire population of the world.

Maybe it did. War is good for business.

I wonder if Mad will see what is to come when she jumps off Mount Baba Dağı and has a clear view of the Mediterranean coastline from Turkey to Israel. Will she see the *feribot, Mavi Marmara*, crossing the water? Will Güzel transfer to her his memory of its decks awash with the blood of Turkish pacifists? Will she look down at the flawed world and understand that her quest for the perfect imperfect is her vocation?

Baba Dagi

*O my lord and my spouse, the hour that I have
longed for has come.* —St. Teresa of Avila

Güzel is becoming anxious. I can smell his sweat, a little different from my own. He does not wear sunscreen. He drinks his
salty *ayran* by the pint in the hot weather. His skin smells of
lemons and milk. *İnşallah.* This is out of our hands. There is a
God or there isn't. The wind will come up to carry us out past
the mountains over the sea, or it won't. Güzel loves me or he
does not. *Bakalım.* None of it matters. In a matter of years, I
will be dust, despite the outcome of this evening's ride. I just
want it to be over so that I can say to myself or someone else can
say about me, "She had the courage to live."

The blood orange sun rests on top of an island in the distance. It may be a Greek island. Any part of Turkey could be
somewhere else. I thought the hills planted with vineyards
around Izmir could have been Sonoma Valley in California.
Now we know the Etruscans came from Smyrna. I come from
Smyrna. I am tricking my mind, keeping it busy with thinking
so that I will not change my mind.

I hum a tune. It is "Paper Doll," my parents' song. My mother sang it over and over after my father died, proving to herself that he still loved her. "*When I come home at night she will be waiting.*" No one is waiting for me on the beach at Ölü-deniz, except possibly the English woman who told me she was too afraid to jump but might change her mind if I did.

Now I know what I am going to do with my father's ashes. I will not drop them into the Mediterranean as planned. I will find a way to smuggle them home with me, maybe in a box of powdery Turkish delight. When I get there, I will buy a soccer ball and fill it with his dust. Then I will take the ball to Ogden Point and kick it into the sea.

Güzel is telling me the story of Ölüdeniz, the beach and lagoon far beneath us. Ölüdeniz means Dead Sea in Turkish. One day, long ago, a father and son who had been out fishing approached the beach in a storm. The son, who was at the helm, insisted on heading for the rocky shore, and the father was equally adamant that they would be dashed on the rocks if they attempted to find shelter in a cove. Desperate to save himself, the father knocked the son overboard with his oar and the son drowned. Just as the boat was about to smash on the rocks, the boat turned into the calm lagoon.

"I will steer us to the lagoon," Güzel says.

When we land, he will step out of the harness and gather up the parachute. He could run off down the beach without looking back. He might lick his lips and taste my sweat. Then he might wipe them the way I did after my father kissed me. Or not. He might swallow and go.

If he does, I will go back to the Sugar Beach Resort, ask to change to a room with a bath instead of a shower, and order a bottle of *raki*. I will take the plastic pouch containing what is left of my father out of my pocket and pack it in my suitcase. Then I will lie in a cool bath and sip the potent anise-tasting liquor, one glass after another, until I fall asleep.

≈

Looking all the way down from the top of Baba Dağı makes me nauseous. I can't tell if I am enamoured with death or taking the easy way out, but at this moment it feels as if it would be easier to jump than go back down the mountain at night. "Why do people take risks like this?"

"I think to have an ecstatic experience, life and death in the same moment."

"So, jumping off the mountain is like falling in love?"

"You never know how it will turn out." My companion smiles at his brutal joke, kicking the dirt on the slope to determine if there is enough wind to fill the parachute. Every time he scuffs his boot in the rocky soil, a thin plume of dust rises and falls. That could be me, deflating at the critical moment. I can only hope it happens over the sea and not on the rocky goat-speckled cliffs below the peak where we are waiting for a warm gust from Africa to fill the 'chute.

Now that the wind has died, I am anxious to jump. Anything would be better than a return trip down the narrow mountain trail. On the way up, I felt the right back wheel spin in the air. I heard rocks fall into the sea. I heard Güzel curse, or was he praying?

"İnşhallah," Güzel shouts from a higher place on the mountain. God go with you. In another life I would be self-conscious. I would worry that he would be repelled by the taste of my salty sweat, my fear; that he would misunderstand. I don't want him to think I am not up to the challenge. I don't want to be a wimp in a country filled with courage. Now, at last, I am beginning to understand Turkey, and maybe myself. Güzel and his countrymen have withstood far more than a fall from a mountain. I know that their unnamed streets and non-linear thinking are passive resistance to every form of violation: social, cultural, geological and political. They live in the moment, because it is the only way to get past fear.

I am not afraid in the way I thought I would be. Now I just want to get it over with. I am sweating because it is hot inside my helmet and combat boots. Even though I have been drinking quarts of water every day during this heat wave from Africa, I rarely pee. No, I am thinking of the Guy Clarke song, "Trust in Your Cape," about little kids who jump off roofs in their Superman costumes. I trust mine. Either it will take me down gently or it will not. I have seen many people die. In the end, they are not afraid. That is what Güzel will taste.

Look what happened to Superman. He broke his neck and died a quadriplegic. Look what happens to all the men and women I have worked with. They die broken and old. The lucky ones forget. For them, life is a free fall. When they go, they jump without parachutes, welcoming the ground that comes up to meet them because they won't remember the pain. I understand that I am the angel who rides with them, just as mine go with me. I won't remember the pain either. Isn't that what Güzel promised?

I looked down on the ride up the mountain and all that fear pinched my heart. Now I am a transparency gazing down at the Aegean, remembering Roman ships coming with Empire builders and Menelaus sailing with his army to claim his adulterous wife on the shores of Troy. What a small fragment of sky I occupy. When I fall, and I will because I intend to jump with or without the help of God or the wind, the space I occupy will immediately fill up.

Whose heart, I wonder, pumps the blood that keeps flowing to my hands and feet, my head? My father's heart failed him and it has failed me as well. If he were standing here right now, wearing this harness with the empty chute lying on the ground behind him, I know what he would have done. He would have given up. The driver would have steered him carefully down the steep goat's path and returned him to his hotel. My father would have tipped heavily and invited his driver to drink *raki* at Ölüdeniz, the beach where restaurants advertise "Proper English Breakfasts." He would have settled into a carpeted banquette at the Help Bar, with the pink Chevrolet with California licence plates stuck halfway through the wall, and the Turkish girls who dance all night, where he would have convinced his new friends that he was a family man. Jumping, he would have insisted, would be irresponsible.

At this moment, when I have too much time to think about what is coming next, I hate my father for leaving us the way he did. What is heart failure but the failure to love? He didn't love my mother and me enough to live. He didn't love us enough to risk life.

For years after he died, I believed he was watching my every move from some heavenly pasture. My mother invoked his presence, beginning every admonition with, "Your father," just as she had done when he was alive. I thought the Our Father at the beginning of school prayers was mine, felt a kind of pride in his being singled out, the prerogative of orphans. "Wait until your father gets home!" my mother said. Slowly, too slowly, I realized that if he were, in fact, my guardian angel then my life would be going better.

My father was nothing more or less than the urn full of ashes my mother kept on her bedside table, probably in the hope that they would transubstantiate into a man with a big erection, while she lay suffering from a widow's erotic longings in her grubby cigarette-burned negligée. She continued to cry out at night and I wondered if she had, indeed, convinced herself that there was an angel in her bed.

The sun is setting on the hills beyond Fethiye, rising again out of the devastation of earthquakes. I have never seen such sunsets. Snow and my father's ashes brought me to Turkey but the sun has melted everything past and present. Memory. Even the Turks are astonished by the heat. Funeral corteges pass through the cobblestone streets every day, sweating men in suits following coffins born by trucks or thin horses pulling carts, with photos of the deceased pinned to their collars like the money attached to the wedding garments of Indian brides doomed to die on their husbands' funeral pyres or live in poverty. My only relief has been taking the *feribots* that cross the harbours of Istanbul and Izmir, drinking the sweet *çay* that is served in glasses and feeling the wind in my face.

The big star slides out of view as quickly as a yolk falls into a mixing bowl. I want to stop it. On this precipice, I should have the power. I should just have to reach out and catch it in my hands. In this country, they use the word *yok* to say "No, not now!" *Yok*! I say to the red yolk settling into the deep blue sea. *Mavi*, the Turks say, the word for the bluest blue I have ever seen. Blue is the colour of their compromised lives, their shops and hotels. They too are as deep as the sea, their secrets hidden in inscrutable waters, like the family heirlooms buried in the Golden Horn. I want to ride the sun into the blue and see what has been hidden from me. I want to see Iman al-Obeidi's face looking fearlessly into the sun from her life prison.

"When the sun goes down, we will have to go back." My real guardian angel digs his fingers into my arms so hard I know I will have bruises. We now have a bond deeper than sexual intimacy. We have felt one another's fear.

"Go, go, go!" he orders, and we run as fast as we can down the rocky hill. I feel his knees bumping into my legs, pushing me forward. His fingers, if possible, dig deeper into my arms.

Abruptly, we are weightless. The wind gathers in our chute and we are flying, as silent as snow. "We are everything and nothing!" I repeat Mustafa's Sufi incantation, gathering my scattered thoughts.

Güzel laughs. I laugh. Our laughter echoes in two parts. I am no longer mortal. Nothing hurts. Nothing weighs me down. We float over the rocky mountain peaks and the goats stop grazing to watch us pass over them.

"Sevmek!" my flight companion shouts. "To love!" I understand. It is a toast. We are on top of the world. It is my turn to give the blessing. I am a snowflake.

The sun hesitates before it disappears behind the silhouette of land into the horizon. The sky shifts from magenta to the most fragile lilac of spring. Little boats bob on the sea. I think I can see the *feribot*, *Mavi Marmara*, on which we crossed the Golden Horn. The sunset is red. The lagoon is as flat as glass. The beach is a bride's ribbon. I am a bride, married to everything I see. I am free.

"Baba Dağı means 'Father Mountain' in Turkish," he yells in my ear. This is my lightness of being.

We hang in the sky for months, years; it couldn't be minutes. I have no way of knowing or caring. Beneath me, the beach and lagoon are as perfect as the day they were made, when the earth moved or lava flowed from its growling belly. Tourists lie in quiet rows on the sand saluting the setting sun, street vendors squeeze lemon on mussels or salt and pepper roasted corn. The band completes their sound check in the palm-roofed club that will come alive with the sound of the blues after dark. The club *is* called Help. It really is. Later, we will spin like dervishes on the dance floor.

"Would you like to rotate?" he asks. What a formal word he has chosen. "Rotate." Before we jumped, after witnessing all kinds of scary air acrobatics, I said, "No tricks, please." This is not a trick. It is the way it is. The world spins. We spin. Dizziness comes from resisting the clockwise movement of life. I get it.

"Yes," I say and, as we turn, sea becomes sky and the sun is not longer round but only one colour in the prism of light.

We spin and I hear Güzel singing. I don't know the words or the music, but deep down I do recognize it. We have come to the centre of the sweet onion spiced with *sumak*, cousin of the poisonous plant. It is not hollow. It is a dome filled with starlight. I am not dizzy. We fly by a flock of the multi-cultural Turkish crow doves, rising to defend their nests in trees on the shoreline. A plane flies over us. It could be Iman in Hillary Clinton's airplane, hopefully leaving her terror and shame behind. I hope so. Do I see her wave from the cockpit, her hands on the controls? All is well, for now. In this moment, balanced in the clear Mediterranean sky, I think we have both found the God we seek, that of which we can conceive nothing greater.

By the time we begin our descent, I neither need Güzel nor love him the way I thought I did. He has been my dear companion. He explains that he will put his feet down first, and on the command "Run" I should stand up and run with him until the 'chute is down and we are safe.

The Mersey grandmother is waiting. It is into her arms that I fall, still running. "Thank God," she says, hugging me so hard and long she could be my sister. "It is all right," I say. "Beautiful." She promises to meet me at the bar after I have changed and rested. She loves the band. Will I tell her everything then? "Yes," I assure her. "There is nothing to be afraid of."

We fold up the parachute and put it in the back of the truck with the harnesses. I take off the boots I rented. The Mersey grandmother says that she photographed several descending paragliders thinking they might be me. She was looking for my girlie shoes but I fooled her with the borrowed boots. She has put her camera away.

"Never mind," I assure her. "I won't need photos to remember this."

I go to my room at the Sugar Beach Club, rows of simple cabins on the lagoon at Ölüdeniz, and shower. No need to change to a room with a bath. No need to buy a bottle of *raki*. I leave my father on the table beside my bed, just where my mother kept him.

⁓

Sarp, the drummer, washboard and slide guitar player from Izmir whose family name means "sharp," is singing. He is the only one in the band not wearing a Panama hat. "*I love to hear that K.C. when she moans/ she sounds like she's got a heavy load.*" The song is about the train *Kansas City*. Two Turkish girls in black dresses, their grey headscarves fallen about their shoulders, sing along as they dance together. I am dancing by myself and I feel as if I have no load at all. I am as light as the air I fell through this afternoon. I open my eyes and see Güzel standing in the back, near the neon club sign, his shadow outlined in electric light.

"My angel," I mouth and wave, and he waves back.

I begin to spin. It feels good and I am not dizzy. The music stops and starts again. Jeff leads off with "Prodigal Son." I spin to the end of the song, and, when I look up, Güzel is gone.

ے۔

Vefa offers to walk me home at the end of the gig. The band is also staying at the Sugar Beach Club. The street is dark at two in the morning and silent, except for the sibilant whispering of cicadas. Neither of us speaks. I am listening for the camels I saw earlier in the day, for their camel breathing and spitting or the rustle of their beige bodies shifting in the night.

Vefa is smoking. I almost comment, but hold back. Turks smoke. They don't understand my North American attitude. Earlier, when Sarp showed off the darkness of his left arm, the suntanned one he rests on the window when he is driving, I asked him if he had any idea of the colour of his lungs. "They are black too," he said, shrugging. "When we have regular earthquakes, volcanoes, droughts and invasions, why would we worry about cigarettes?" Why indeed.

Vefa's holder is an odd touch of elegance in his otherwise casual presentation – baseball cap, jeans and T-shirts. The holder, for some reason, marks him as a deep thinker. He translates philosophical writing. His father is a poet. Vefa is a manchild, waifish and yet sophisticated, a shape Coon might have grown into.

A motorcycle speeds by. There is a girl in high heels riding bitch. "Sweet Papa Lowdown," the driver cries out, catching Vefa's instrument case in the beam of his headlight, and the girl repeats after him.

"That is fame," I say.

"It's that ephemeral, a voice in the night that drives away," Vefa agrees. "So long as we don't chase after it, we are OK. The voice can never be found again."

He is right and, after this afternoon, I am ready to hear him say such a thing without feeling grief. I touched the sky and I heard beautiful music. It is all done, and the fact of its ending doesn't make any of it less perfect.

"Shhh," I whisper, and point to the pomegranate grove where the camels were resting when I walked by on my way to Ölüdeniz yesterday morning. The trees are still. We walk closer. I am careful in my platform shoes. There is manure scattered around.

"They are gone," I say. "Where could they be?"

∼

When I woke up this morning, I found a Turkish newspaper at the end of my bed. At the bottom of the front page is a story circled in pencil. I can't read it but I do make out the words Iman and Libya. There is a photo from better days, perhaps when she graduated from law school. Iman is smiling at the camera. She is somewhere in America and I am here, both of us found, although not where I thought we would be.

I was sure Güzel would disappear, one way or the other. I have googled the Turkish police and found reports of torture and other human rights abuses. Are these stories true or do the

Iranians and the Syrians make them up for political reasons? I didn't imagine that Pamuk and other writers have been arrested for insulting Turkishness. What could Güzel have done to warrant his disappearance?

In the Turkey I have seen, men with humble businesses dig deep into their cash registers for poor beggars, people will stop what they are doing to guide visitors five hundred metres in the right direction, and a complete stranger will offer to share his food or his bed to a visitor. Do these kind and civilized people really torture one another?

The old me would have rushed to the *jandarma* station and reported Güzel missing. I would have gone to the end of the earth, probably Mount Ararat where life began, or began again, and shouted his name as Greenpeace volunteers loaded the animals two by two onto the new Ark. I would have put up "Man Missing" signs along with the Sweet Papa Lowdown posters I have been taping to every available surface. I would have attempted to locate his family, and I would have informed the newspapers, "He was there one moment and then he wasn't." I translated my statement into Turkish and that made me laugh. I smelled orange blossoms.

Güzel is not lost. I am found, home at last with my dad's ashes and a bottle of Turkish orange blossom jam. Every now and again, I smell electricity and think of Haydarpasa Station, the crossroads of Europe and Asia, where the Orient Express meets trains to Asia and the ferries that cross the Bosphorus. When I heard that there had been an electrical fire at Haydarpasa, I wondered if I was psychic and if that was the fire of parthenogenesis, God's weary finger reaching out for a last try at humanity. Perhaps.

VICTORIA

Recently, I watched *Shall We Dance* on television. It was late at night but Fred and Ginger kept me awake. I love her infamous gaucheries and Fred trying not to show exasperation, the benign expression my father wore for my graceless mother. In the middle of "They Can't Take That Away from Me," Fred dropped Ginger and stepped out of the television set, gliding across the room to where I waited for him to take me in his arms.

"What do you know, kiddo?" my father asked, as I stepped onto his patent leather shoes and finished the dance. "How was Turkey?"

"I think I found you," I answered, meaning myself.

"Now you're getting it," my dad said, making a *one, two, three,* reverse turn and disappearing into the night.

ele

The Turks have a present perfect tense for conjecture. It is called "*mis*" with a cedilla, which I do not have on my computer, under the "s." I might say, "Once upon a time I knew a man called Güzel," the verb ending revealing that I did not actually meet him in the reality we know as now. How beautiful are the semantics of innuendo, which allow the Turks to distinguish between "maybe" and "certainly." It is the language of storytelling. Visitors have a hard time comprehending that. Maybe they are their own genre, a separate but parallel reality. Do we find romance in the uncertainty of English, maddening as it might be in a court of law? Do I, or do I not actually imagine this? Isn't everything we perceive just perception? Thank you, Aristotle and Bishop Berkeley.

This is the lesson of the Arab Spring, which decanted the old regimes only to create a hollow space, a place for insanity, where *jihad* bloodies the sand on Libya's beautiful coastline, and where, according to recent reports from Colorado where Iman al-Obeidi is in jail for assault, she is not adjusting well to her own post-traumatic reality, life in "freedomland."

اﻪ

How far was it down the mountain? I write back, knowing it was more than five hundred metres, knowing Güzel will smile sadly because he knew the comforting memory of the *saz* and warm snow falling on my shoulders was magical thinking, temporary distraction from seismic rumblings and ashes, the new caliphate.

I wonder if, trumpet in hand, my apostate angel will be waiting for me at Dabiq, where I intend to find him again.

"Would you believe I found a ruby in my breakfast eggs today?" Could you please tell my father?

GLOSSARY OF TURKISH WORDS

Ağrı Dağı: Mount Ararat

Ayran: whipped yogurt, garlic, salt and water, a refreshing drink, especially in the heat.

Baba Dağı: Father Mountain in Southwestern Turkey

Bakalım: we shall see

Beyoğlu: the international district of Istanbul, a hub of Mediterranean trade

bozuk: broken

bozuk para: coins

bozdurmak: change saved by storekeepers for the poor, who are welcome to claim it

çay: tea, a key to understanding the linguistic relationship between Asian and Middle Eastern countries influenced by Islam, where çay is a common word from Istanbul to Delhi

çok güzel: meaning full of goodness, a common expression for "terrific."

dolmuş: Turkish buses which depart when full, like "stuffed" grape leaves.

feribot: ferry boat, essential transportation in Adriatic harbours

hajib: covering garment worn by Muslim women.

hamam: a steam bath

İnşallah: go with God, a blessing

iptal: cancelled

İstiklal Caddesi: main street in Beyoğlu, Istanbul

Jandarma: police

jihad: holy war

Kadıköy: Asian district of Istanbul. The hotel where Mad stayed was also the destination of the wife of the Paris kosher grocery bomber in 2015.

Kitan – the circumcision ceremony. Young boys on the cusp of adolescence, dressed like princes and prepared for manhood, are celebrated on this day.

kitapçı: bookseller

kuku: female genitals

lokum: turkish delight, gelatin candy

mavi: blue, a well-used word in a country defined by blue sky and bright seas

Merhaba: good day, a greeting

mezze: small plates of appetizers that precede a meal

Mevlevi Sema: Sufi dervish ceremony, banned under the secular regime but recently rehabilitated as a tourist attraction

minerale su: mineral water

orospu: prostitute

Ölüdeniz: dead sea lagoon area near Fetiye

pasajı: covered market

piliç: chicken or "chick" when referring to young women

portakal suyu: orange juice, su meaning "water."

Qur'an: Muslim holy book, the Koran.

rakı: anise liquor. In Turkey, there has been tolerance toward alcohol consumption, but that is changing.

Sarayı: a palace

saz: a stringed instrument

simit: doughnut or bagel shaped bread with seeds, sold by street vendors, some of whom carry trays with dozens on their heads

sofrası: buffet restaurant

Sultanahmet: historic district of Istanbul where Topkapı Palace, the Aya Sofia and the Blue Mosque are situated

sumak: an acidic spice

teşekkur: thanks

tünel: underground rail car in Beyo lu, which takes passengers from the waterfront to the top of the hill

tuvalet kağıdı: toilet paper

yabancı: foreigner

Yok!: Get lost!

ACKNOWLDEGMENTS

Thanks to those who are showing compassion and welcoming refugees from the horror in the Middle East, the hundreds of thousands who kept on caring about Iman al-Obeidi and the sanctity of life, even after she, like the Arab Spring, broke under pressure, and thanks to Sarp Keskiner, Vefa Karatay, Tugrul Aray, Berk Sirman and Cagdas Dinc, musicians and Ottoman philosophers, the Department of External Affairs, Sweet Papa Lowdown, Jeff Shucard, Doug Rhodes and Kris Bowerman, The Pink Harem, Naomi and Hannah Shucard and Françoise Levesque, Sinan and Selda Sakizli and Baykus Studio, Eva and Jack, who shared one Turkish journey, John Trigg, Balkan specialist with British Intelligence, Halkan Akdere, who blessed my shoulders and guided me down the mountain, Musa Dagdeviren, chef and owner of Ciya Sofrası and keeper of Turkish tradition, and Mandoturk, aka Rick van Krugel, who flies on a magic carpet when he is playing music and always lands on the right notes.

And with gratitude to Exile Editions: Barry and Michael Callaghan, Gabriela Campos, and Nina Callaghan, for their transformations.

Linda Rogers of Victoria, B.C. is a broadcaster, teacher, journalist, poet, novelist and songwriter. For fiction and poetry she has received 10 writing awards. Her journalistic work ranges from reviews, interviews and critical essays about literary, musical, dance and visual artists. She has edited several anthologies, and her work has been translated worldwide. She has served as President of the League of Canadian Poets and the B.C. Federation of Writers and was Canada's Peoples' Poet in 2000.